IF THAT DOG HAD A SUITCASE

By Jackie Goddard

Front cover illustration by Jon Haward

CHAPTER ONE

The distant roar from upstairs silenced everyone round the breakfast table.

Even baby Rory, who had been sitting quietly in his high-chair filling his nappy, stopped in mid-strain and they all waited with bated breath for the storm to break.

It came in the form of footsteps thundering down the stairs, then the kitchen door flew open and clouds of sheets, duvet covers and other assorted laundry were hurled into the room from an invisible source.

The footsteps receded, and as they thumped up the stairs again, Tom picked a stiffened sock out of his cornflakes and pushed the bowl aside.

He raised an eyebrow at the two older children and Jade and Lee stared back at him, shrugging their shoulders in unison.

Tom sighed deeply and shook his head while their cowardly old Great Dane, Sophie, put one enormous paw across her eyes and whimpered as they waited for the next phase.

When Annie barged into the kitchen at last her fury was almost tangible.

She banged a tray down on the table that was laden with an assortment of furry cups, bowls and glasses, while in her other hand was a wastepaper bin that overflowed with crisp packets, mouldy apple cores and blackened banana skins.

Without saying a word she dumped the bin in Jade's lap, then snatched up the laundry and went into the utility room, crashing the door shut behind her.

"Would this be a good time to ask for our pocket money do you think?" Lee whispered with a grin.

He got a cuff round the ear from his dad, a swift kick in the shin from Jade and an earful of porridge, flicked by Rory.

"I'll take that as a 'no' then," he said quickly, as his mum reappeared with a pile of clean bed linen.

"Upstairs NOW, both of you," she snarled "and you're grounded for a fortnight."

She exited without waiting for a response, leaving a chill breeze in her wake.

Before Jade and Lee could even think of begging their dad for mercy they heard the utility room door open again and turned to see Aunt Lizzie peering warily round the corner.

"I was only looking for a spare pillow," the old lady sniffed "and she shut me in the airing cupboard".

A couple of hours later Annie was happy with the world once more, out in her garden.

They lived in an old farmhouse on a mainly disused farm just half a mile from the village, which meant it was very peaceful most of the time, but within easy walking distance for the pub and local amenities when required. It was a far cry from how things were when she and Tom had met in London almost twenty years ago, both with busy, quite stressful jobs, staying in poky little flats and joining in with the rat race. When they got married they'd taken the decision to get out of the city and so had moved to Scotland, where Annie had been brought up, and they had never regretted it. Tom was a fantastic husband, had the patience of a saint, as well as a wicked sense of humour and barely a day went by when they didn't find something to laugh about.

Annie loved her life and she loved her family above all else. Although they were not financially well off and had known some tough times, they had come through it with the help and support of family and friends, so as far as she was concerned, they were richer by far than many people she knew.

She also loved the fact that her dad and her sister both lived nearby, her dad in a little house in the village and her sister Kate on a farm about five miles away. Sadly, they had lost her precious mum to cancer some years earlier, an event that had devastated them all as it had happened so quickly, but they had managed to get through it by being there for each other, as always.

One positive thing to have happened at that time was that her mum's sister, Aunt Lizzie, had come to stay with them to help and afterwards had been persuaded to stay for good. She was now a permanent fixture in their lives, a funny, feisty, no-nonsense character who loved her sister's mad family and took everything in her stride. She also did more than her share of chores and housework, so was considered by all of them, especially Annie, to be their fairy godmother.

Aunt Lizzie had also, initially, been a great source of comfort to Annie's dad, who had taken his wife's death particularly hard. They had spent many hours reminiscing over their shared memories, and gradually the healing process had begun for both of them.

Nowadays they had a very sparky friendship with a lot of banter and insults on both sides that would have people who didn't know them convinced they didn't like each other, but the family knew differently and thoroughly enjoyed the double act they often provided.

After her mini explosion that morning Annie had despatched everyone else to the nearby town to do the weekly food shop and, since it was a thirty-mile round trip, she could be assured of two or three hours peace and quiet.

Having decided that she'd done enough housework to salve her conscience for a week she was now kneeling between the rows of newly sprouting peas, hidden by a small trellis fence and enjoying the feel of the warm soft soil between her fingers as she delicately weeded between the little plants.

She became aware of a distant drone and looked up to see a tractor on the opposite hill, ploughing slowly across the field and looking for all the world like a giant sewing machine, with hundreds of seagulls dropping behind like big white stitches.

Annie savoured the moment and felt all the tension of the morning seeping away, so after watching for a few more minutes she returned to her task.

Just as she was nearing the end of her second row she heard the squeak of the gate and a high-pitched whistle that heralded her dad's approach up the garden.

He had worn a hearing aid for many years now but had never quite mastered the volume switch so was forever trying to adjust it, unaware that to those nearby it sounded as if he was piping himself aboard.

Annie heard him muttering to himself,

"Bloody stupid contraption," he cursed "one minute I can hear the dog fart at the end of the garden and the next ………."

His daughter suddenly popped her head up above the trellis,

"Having a bit of trouble there Dad?" she bellowed.

There was a clatter as the old man dropped the hoe he'd been carrying and jumped two feet in the air.

Annie helped him indoors, put the kettle on and thought about offering him a paper bag to breathe into.

"I thought you buggers were all out," he said at last, accepting his tea with a trembling hand, "I was just going to weed the cabbages."

"I reckon you almost manured them there as well," Annie muttered under her breath.

"I bloody well heard that," said her dad, whose hearing aid was now at full volume and lying on the kitchen table.

After their tea break the old man went back to the garden and started hoeing furiously, while having a fairly animated conversation with himself and Annie watched him from the kitchen window, smiling fondly.

He was a fiercely independent man with his own set of rules, was very definitely not afraid to speak his mind and had no time for people who couldn't just say what they meant so he was known as a bit of a character in the village. But for all his tough exterior and seemingly grumpy nature, his family meant the world to him and he would do anything for them – he was especially proud of his five grandchildren and liked to spoil them whenever he got the chance. They were all quite used to his gruff manner as well and weren't the slightest bit afraid of him, although some of their friends were often very wary when he appeared.

He also liked to spend a lot of time in their garden, which was an enormous help to Annie as it was so big she wouldn't have managed it on her own, so she was *nearly* always pleased to see him cycle down the lane almost every day.

When the gang returned from town they found that Annie had prepared lunch, much to everyone's amazement, because once the gardening season arrived it was a rare occurrence for her to remember such mundane things as meals, let alone prepare them.

"Don't get too excited," she warned them all "there's a chore list for afters."

Aunt Lizzie had gone to tell Grandad that lunch was ready but when she came back she was positively bristling with indignation.

"The daft old sod has just accused me of sneaking up on him," she fumed "he dropped his hoe and swore at me."

Through the window Annie could see her dad hanging on to the fence with one hand and his chest with the other.

"He'll be fine once his heart kicks in again" she observed.

CHAPTER TWO

Two hours later Tom was standing on the roof with his eyes tightly shut and hugging the chimney stack like a long-lost friend, while cursing a few things under his breath.

He cursed the fact that they had an open fire, that the roof was covered in very dodgy tiles, that he had no head for heights and, worst of all, a terrible memory. Otherwise he would have remembered to buy some new rods, after discovering last winter that they'd been chewed through by something like a beaver, judging by the state of them.

On that occasion he had clambered up onto the frosty, slippery roof with the weighted brush and by the time he'd finished he'd lost a few pounds in weight, gained a lot of grey hairs and found religion.

Now here he was again – and most of all he cursed the fact that he had not recognised the danger signs when he'd been sitting in the garden with Annie just half an hour ago.

He cast his mind back to that peaceful spell they'd been enjoying, sitting in their favourite spot in a corner where the shrubs, ferns and flowers had been allowed to grow wild, thereby forming a perfect screen from the rest of the garden.

It was a place they both liked to escape to on occasion and after lunch he had persuaded his wife to take a break there for a while.

Aunt Lizzie had stomped off to the village, pushing Rory in his buggy, after declaring she'd been abused and insulted enough for one day.

Lee was busy chopping kindling in the coal shed, Jade had been presented with a huge pile of ironing and Grandad was lurking somewhere in the vegetable garden, still not talking to anyone.

So, they'd been sitting there quietly for a while, eyes closed and enjoying the warmth of the sun on their faces with nothing but the sound of birds, droning bees and the chugging of a distant tractor to disturb the tranquillity.

It was at times like this that Tom's thoughts often went back to the years he'd worked as a salesman, and how much pressure that involved, trying to meet targets every month in order to earn a bonus, sometimes having to spend several nights a week away from his family. It was hard to believe how very different his life was now in his job as a youth worker, one that gave him immense satisfaction, and also meant that he was able to come home every night to what he considered to be a little corner of heaven, albeit quite a crazy one at times, but he wouldn't change it for the world.

Twenty minutes later a rustle in the bushes at the far end of the garden had caused Tom to open his eyes and peer through the curtain of ferns. He saw Sophie emerge, look furtively round and then trot across the lawn with her head held high.

"What the hell has that dog got in her mouth?" he whispered to his wife.

Annie squinted in the same direction for a moment.

"I think it's the rabbit," she replied.

Tom peered even harder,

"Do you reckon it's OK?"

"She's just taking it for a walk, it'll be fine – with that dog's breath the rabbit's probably comatose by now anyway, won't remember a thing."

"Yeah, you're probably right" he said, then they both closed their eyes again and tilted their faces to the sun.

Ten minutes later Tom had been dreaming of blue skies, golden sand and waves crashing on to the beach, while his wife heard the washing machine go into its final spin and the sound of a plate smashing as it fell off the vibrating sink unit.

She'd begun to fidget.

That precise moment was when Tom made his big mistake. That was when he should have made a break for his workshop to fix the lawnmower. But instead he had tried to stretch the moment out a little longer – and then he'd heard the fateful words,

"It's about time that bloody chimney was swept again."

So here he was, clinging on for dear life, waiting for his heart to resume a normal rhythm and fully aware that he now had an audience.

"I bet the view is fantastic up there on a day like this" Annie called from below.

She was too far away to hear his muttered reply and he had no intention of looking down to see if her tongue was in her cheek.

"Why the hell didn't he get some new rods and clean it from the inside like any normal bloke would do?" Grandad was asking no one in particular "those slates are dangerous – he'll break his bloody neck one day."

"It's being so cheerful that keeps you going, you old goat," countered Aunt Lizzie, just back from the village "keep your voice down will you."

Tom felt a tile move beneath his foot and clung on tighter still, feeling sweat trickling down his back.

"If he'd remembered to get the rods, I could have done the job for him" Grandad continued grimly.

"Go and make a pot of tea will you dad" suggested Annie.

The old man shuffled off, much to Tom's relief, but when he finally opened his eyes he then saw Cinders the cat eyeing him up from the nearby tree and he could tell from her sneering expression that she had no more faith in him than Grandad.

She was one of the most malevolent creatures they had ever known and she hated everyone with a passion, apart from Jade. Most of her life was spent lying in wait for the opportunity to frighten the wits out of people by jumping out at them, hissing and spitting.

Her run-ins with Sophie had been pretty spectacular as well, when she usually left the poor dog reduced to a quivering wreck, but they reckoned she was worth her keep because she was more of a guard dog than Sophie would ever be. She also had a peculiar habit of sleeping in the tumble drier from time to time which they had to be wary of, but they had so far resisted the temptation to switch it on while she was in it.

Tom tore his eyes away from her hypnotic gaze and realised that the view was indeed spectacular – but that he still preferred it from the ground, so he quickly dropped the weighted brush down the chimney, hauled it up and down a few times and then made his way down the ladder.

"You're a star," said Annie, handing him a can of lager "I know how much you hate going up there."

Tom took a long, long drink and reflected, not for the first time, that it wasn't the going up that troubled him really – it was the thought of coming down again at very high speed that brought him out in a cold sweat.

At teatime they had a barbecue – a request that Tom was happy to comply with because it meant he could stand still for an hour or so.

Grandad was being his usual optimistic self as he watched Tom's preparations.

"You'll never get that to light," he grumbled "the wood's too damp."

Tom ignored him and continued to build a framework of kindling on top of some screwed up paper, then he put a layer of charcoal on and set light to it.

Much to Grandad's disgust it caught instantly and very soon the coals were glowing red.

"It won't last five minutes, you'd better get the sausages on quick."

"It's not ready yet," said Tom "the coals have to be white before you start cooking."

"Stuff and bloody nonsense, it'll have gone out by then," said the old man "I've got just the thing you need in the car."

He disappeared for a few minutes but on his return was swearing profusely, having stepped in one of Sophie's dollops en route.

"That's the only dog I know who can crap on a par with a Clydesdale horse," he cursed "this garden's like a bloody minefield."

He stood scuffing his shoe on the grass and eyeing the barbecue with great suspicion.

When the coals were ready Jade was sent in to fetch the meat and gather everyone else together because Tom could see that Grandad was edging closer and almost twitching with anticipation, so he felt it unwise to leave the old man alone with a gallon can of petrol.

Some time later they were all relaxing after the feast, mostly sprawled out on the grass but with the two oldies seated in comfy armchairs, when the noise of an approaching vehicle caused them to look up the lane and they saw a battered old van coming into the farmyard.

Tom walked towards the gate as two very large, scruffy looking men got out, one of whom strolled off in the direction of the barn, while the other walked towards the house.

"Got any old furniture you don't want, mate" he called loudly.

Tom was polite but short when he replied they had nothing of interest.

"Oh, I'm sure there must be some odds and ends lying about" the man persisted, lifting the latch of the gate as he spoke.

"I wouldn't do that if I were you" said Tom quietly, while at the same moment there was a rustle from the tree above and the intruder suddenly found himself wearing a grey fur collar and staring eyeball to yellow eyeball with Cinders.

As the man let out a yell of terror Sophie came hurtling round the corner of the house, barking furiously and ran straight past him into the yard.

The second man saw her thundering towards him and, since she was between him and the van, he started running hell for leather up the lane.

This was like a red rag to a bull for Sophie who, despite her cowardice, was not fond of strangers so she chased after him at full tilt until she was close enough to ram him in the backside with her nose.

Such was her size and speed that she actually lifted him off the ground and carried him for a few feet, he with his legs still going like pistons, before dropping him unceremoniously onto the grass verge.

In the meantime, Tom had managed to disentangle Cinders from the first man who had jumped back into the van, put his foot to the floor and sped up the lane, barely slowing down enough for his mate to dive into the passenger seat.

Sophie strolled back down the lane to a round of applause then went straight to the centre of the garden and dropped an enormous dollop.

"I reckon she's making a statement there" Tom laughed.

"Looks more like she's had a shit on the lawn to me" said Grandad.

CHAPTER THREE

The following morning Annie woke to the sound of Tom's strangled coughing, caused by Rory having used him as a trampoline when he'd clambered out of his cot by their bed.

Tom refused her offer of a cup of tea, wiped the tears from his eyes and rolled over to go back to sleep so Annie took Rory to the kitchen, strapped him in his highchair and gave him his cereal.

By the time she'd had a quick wash and got dressed Rory was finished. Annie wiped the porridge off the walls and the dog, changed Rory's nappy then took him back to snuggle in beside his dad with a bottle.

As a precaution she also fixed the safety gate outside the door because, although Rory was only ten months old, he was already managing to take a few doddery little steps and had a great spirit of adventure.

Since it was still only 6am Annie decided to take advantage of the time to herself and went out to weed a few more rows of vegetables, but while she worked she jotted down the chore list for the day.

These lists were a standing joke in the family but for Annie they were a lifeline. She had such a bad memory and was so easily distracted that she could not survive without them, so the family were now quite used to the daily list, with names written beside each chore.

There were also times when they got their own back by leaving little notes for her, such as:

'What day of the week is dinner?'

'Change Rory's nappy – PLEASE'

and on odd occasions when she'd been working late in the garden till it was too dark to see she would find a note from Tom saying,

'Put the bloody lights out and come to bed!'

Annie didn't mind really, she was just glad the family could see the funny side of it and they were all perfectly capable of running the house without her interference.

This pleased her greatly because she detested housework in all forms, not only because she found it incredibly boring, but the fact that she was supposed to go through the same stupid routine almost daily drove her to distraction – hence her explosion of the previous morning.

After a couple of hours Annie went indoors for breakfast and as she entered the kitchen, she heard a distant yell and a crash. Moments later Tom hobbled through with Rory waddling behind him in hot pursuit.

"Some bloody safety gate," he complained "I nearly broke my neck."

"Silly bugger" said Annie.

Her husband limped off for a shower, closely followed by Rory, who like to sit in the end of the bath and just plodge.

Annie munched her way through a bacon sandwich and scanned her soil stained list.

Most of Tom's chores were fairly regular ones because nearly every gadget in the house was old and clapped out so he just kept repairing them as well as he could until they finally gave up the ghost.

Regular visitors thought nothing of watching Annie kick start the washing machine or knock seven bells out of the microwave to get it going but as far as she was concerned there was no point in buying new while they could still get things working, however unorthodox the method.

When Tom returned he was ready for breakfast so he got the frying pans out for his weekly 'cholesterol special', at which point Annie made a quick exit because she knew the kitchen was about to be reduced to a shambles.

For all her faults in the housework department she was very methodical when she cooked and always washed up as she went along, whereas Tom used every utensil in the kitchen and waited till after he'd eaten to clear up.

For this reason Annie had made it clear many years ago that whoever cooked did their own dishes, including the children, and since Jade appeared to be following in her father's footsteps in her style of cooking, she felt this was justified.

Instead of going back outside Annie went into the study to get on with some of her writing. Next to gardening this was her favourite pastime and so far, she had written a short children's book for Jade and Lee when they were small, a few dozen humorous poems and at present she was working on a novel, based not too loosely on her own mad family. She had also discovered a talent for writing personalised poetry for any occasion and was happy to be able to earn some extra cash from her commissions.

Originally, she had used a good old-fashioned typewriter, as she was a self-confessed technophobe, but the family had finally persuaded her to get to grips with the basics of a computer which, she reluctantly had to agree, did make the job so much quicker and easier.

However, she stubbornly refused to have anything to do with the Internet, Facebook, Twitter or anything that involved going online, declaring that she did not need to know about 'the world and his wife' or any of their problems.

She felt the same about mobile phones, and while she recognised their usefulness in certain situations, she was perfectly happy with the ancient 'brick' of a phone that Tom had passed on to her years ago. Annie always had it switched on and charged but it rarely rang as she had very few contacts in it and she hated texting as it took her ages, so she hardly ever replied to them either. To begin with she'd kept it in her 'Mary Poppins' bag, but it used to take her so long to find it when it did ring occasionally that the caller had hung up, so nowadays she kept it tucked into her bra.

As her fingers flew over the keyboard the smell of frying bacon wafted through the house and soon after she heard sounds of movement from above, which meant that Lee was awake and ready for breakfast.

She heard his door open, followed by a swooshing noise, then a thud.

When she went into the hall Lee was lying flat on his back, slightly winded.

His mum stood over him, hands on hips.

"I'll never get the hang of that banister" he groaned.

From above another door opened and Jade appeared, taking in the situation as she glided down the stairs. She stepped over her brother with barely a glance.

"Dozy pillock" was her only comment as she continued down the hall.

Aunt Lizzie came through from her room at that point and gazed down at Lee.

"My bum hurts" he moaned.

The old lady looked up at Annie.

"He hasn't really got both oars in the water has he" she said, then she too went off to have her breakfast.

Annie thought the two of them had summed things up quite nicely, so she said nothing and went back to her computer.

By late morning Annie felt she'd done well enough to take a break, so she went out to see what the rest of them were up to.

The children had filled the paddling pool and Aunt Lizzie was seated in her favourite armchair, feet in the water, listening to music through her headphones and knitting like fury.

The armchair was one of two that had been intended for the dump some time ago, but the old lady had claimed them for the garden for her and Grandad, because she refused to sit on the plastic chairs the others used.

"Bloody awful things," she'd maintained "sit on them for half an hour and you lose the use of your legs, then when you do stand up they nearly rip your skin off"

Aunt Lizzie's passion was knitting and she was rarely seen without her needles and balls of wool, no matter where she was.

Since first coming to live with them she had knitted countless jumpers, scarves, gloves and bobble hats for all the family, as well as hundreds of squares which she made up into patchwork blankets and donated to charity. Nowadays she concentrated on knitting jumpers for Rory, as well as Kate's two little ones, Adam and Amy.

At the moment she was listening to one of Annie's party tapes, nodding in time to the music and with her needles almost smouldering from the speed she was knitting at.

Tom was nowhere to be seen so Annie guessed he'd be tinkering in his workshop.

Her dad had also arrived at some stage and was back in the vegetable garden with his hoe, keeping a wary eye out for anyone sneaking up on him.

Annie was just about to creep away and go back to her computer when Aunt Lizzie suddenly threw her knitting to the ground and pulled off her headphones.

"Damn and blast," she swore "I can go like the clappers to Meatloaf and Bon Jovi but Bob Marley makes me drop all my stitches."

"I guess that would explain his hats then." said Annie

Lunch was a mountain of very peculiar sandwiches, prepared by Aunt Lizzie and looked upon with great suspicion by Grandad.

"I'll just have the lettuce and onion, thanks" said Tom.

Lee opted for ham and banana, Jade chose tuna and grapes and Annie took her cheese and marmalade ones indoors because she preferred them toasted – Rory sucked happily on half a cucumber and a rusk while Grandad followed her to make his own.

"That woman's as daft as a brush" the old man complained, as he buttered two slices of bread and sprinkled one liberally with sugar.

"She means well," said Annie "and the children like them."

Her dad spread a layer of cream cheese on the second slice then slapped the two together, looking at Annie's toasted creation in disgust,

"Don't know how you can eat that muck" he said as left the kitchen.

An hour or so later and after a short siesta it was time to get back to work.

Aunt Lizzie had become increasingly irritated by Grandad's snoring and had woken him by squirting him in the ear with a water pistol, so he'd jumped on his bike and pedalled off home, cursing.

Tom stretched, yawned and then sighed as he saw Annie bearing down on him with her grubby piece of paper.

"Right then," he said, without much enthusiasm "what's left on my list?"

His wife grinned and announced,

"Ballcock and dollops."

"Sounds like a firm of solicitors" said Tom.

CHAPTER FOUR

Monday morning got off to a bad start when a power cut in the night meant that the alarm clock didn't go off, but fortunately Rory was sick on Tom's head in time to wake them with just half an hour to spare.

They spent that time in complete pandemonium with everyone charging round the house like a video on fast forward and with Jade only adding to the tension by hogging the bathroom for most of it.

Tom was going to be late for an appointment and was furious that he'd only managed a three minute shower and a very quick shave, he was convinced his daughter had spent most of her time in there reading,

"Those bloody magazines have got to go" had been his parting shot, as he'd grabbed his car keys and dashed out of the house.

Because he'd been so stroppy Annie hadn't bothered to tell him about the blood spots on his collar and the lump of shaving foam in his ear.

After watching Jade and Lee run up the lane for the school bus Annie turned to survey the chaos of the kitchen.

She heaved a deep sigh, took Rory back to bed for his nap and went outside to do more weeding. Aunt Lizzie appeared an hour or so later with tea and toast, knowing full well that Annie would not have had breakfast.

"Kitchen's done" she said, handing over the plate.

Annie gave her a grateful smile and felt a slight twinge of guilt because she'd guessed the old lady would clear up once she had the house to herself. It was only a mild twinge though, because Annie knew that Aunt Lizzie enjoyed keeping busy and making herself useful.

"The hoover's knackered though – it's not picking up and it sounds like a tank."

"No problem" said Annie "I'll fix it later."

The two women sat and chatted for a while about nothing in particular until Grandad arrived on his bike with steam coming out of his ears.

It turned out that he'd been cycling through the village when the postman had jumped out of his van without looking and knocked him clean off his bike.

If he'd been looking for sympathy, he was to be disappointed.

Both women thought it was hilarious and only laughed even harder when he went on to tell them that after picking himself up and giving the postman a mouthful of abuse he'd cycled on a bit further until the coalman had leapt down from his lorry and knocked him off again.

By the time he'd finished his sorry tale Aunt Lizzie and Annie had tears streaming down their cheeks, so he stormed off to the kitchen to make himself a cup of tea.

"You're a bunch of nutters, the lot of you," he shouted across the lawn at them "this whole bloody family's mad."

Aunt Lizzie mopped her face and said weakly

"We'd never survive if we weren't."

When Rory woke from his nap Annie took him for a quick dunk in the bath with her, then got them both ready for town.

She had arranged to meet her sister for lunch to discuss arrangements for the forthcoming christening. Kate was a nurse and married to a farmer, they already had a two year old son, Adam, but she had discovered she was pregnant again with Amy shortly before Rory was born so they'd agreed to wait and have both babies done as a job lot.

After putting the finishing touches to her make-up Annie went outside to let the old ones know she was leaving.

She stuck her head out of the door and realised there was a slanging match going on.

Apparently Sophie had managed to rip open a rubbish sack and the contents of it were now strewn across the lawn, while the culprit was cowering under a bush at the end of the garden.

"You stupid old goat" Aunt Lizzie was yelling "you should have been watching her."

"She's not my bloody dog" Grandad shouted back "and anyway, you should put your rubbish bags out of her reach."

Annie got a fresh sack and started picking all the litter up, noting as she did so that Sophie was now creeping slowly across the grass on her belly in a bid to get back to the house.

It always amused them that their enormous jet black hound seemed to think that she couldn't be seen when she did this and Annie was very tempted to wait till she could see the whites of Sophie's eyes and then yell "BOO" at her, but she was in too much of a hurry to have to resuscitate the daft animal so she resisted.

By the time she'd dumped the sack in the coal shed and strapped Rory into his car seat Sophie had made it to the back door.

She hung her huge head over the gate and was possibly trying to give Annie an apologetic smile but only succeeded in looking as though she was just coming round from an anaesthetic.

Her dad and Aunt Lizzie were now ignoring each other from opposite ends of the garden so Annie jumped into the car and gave them a farewell toot, thinking that any visitors or would-be salesmen who might arrive in her absence would probably wish they'd never got out of bed that morning.

Kate was already in the Chinese restaurant when they arrived, which was no surprise to Annie as her sister was by far the more organised of the two of them, even though she was the younger. She tried her best to keep Annie on track and even kept a diary for her, reminding her of important dates like dental appointments, parent's nights, birthdays and such, which Annie was always grateful for because she rarely remembered to check her own calendar.

After ordering their meal they got straight down to making lists on their napkins as Kate only had a couple of hours before she picked Adam up from day care. While Amy slept like an angel Rory used some chopsticks and the tray of his high chair as a drum kit, pausing only occasionally to spit sweetcorn into his mum's char sui.

"He's not fond of lumps yet" explained Annie.

"Not a bad aim though" her sister replied.

By the time they ordered dessert they were satisfied that everyone knew what they were doing for the christening, so Annie then related the tale of their dad's escapade that morning.

After wiping away her tears Kate, in turn, said that he'd been up to their farm a few days earlier, adjusting his bike, and that she was a bit concerned about the safety of it now.

"I'm sure his brakes are dodgy" she said "but he's also set it in permanent top gear now as well – we gave him a lift back to make sure he got home safely, at least this once."

"I expect he thinks it will make the uphill journey to your place a bit easier now" said Annie.

"Yes, but it's downhill all the way back," Kate pointed out "not to mention that steep hill just at the start of the village."

They paused in their eating – each of them with their own mental picture of a turbo charged pensioner flying straight down the high street with his face contorted by the G-force.

"And there's the river at the other end" Annie remembered.

"He's coming up again tomorrow" said Kate.

They were silent again for a moment until Annie remarked,

"If you could only persuade him to wear a cape and mask, I could sell tickets."

They weren't exactly thrown out of the restaurant, but while they were both having hysterics Rory lobbed a banana fritter into their neighbour's chop suey, so they felt it best to pay the bill quickly and leave.

Back home again all was peaceful.

Grandad had gone home and Aunt Lizzie was dozing in her armchair in the greenhouse, where it was usually stored until Tom heaved it out on to the lawn for her.

She had fallen asleep with needles poised in mid-stitch, so Annie checked the thermometer to make sure the old lady wasn't likely to overcook and left her snoring a while longer.

As it was almost time for the school bus Annie decided against gardening and went inside to overhaul the clapped out old hoover while Rory amused himself in his playpen.

She was on her knees in the sitting room, peering into the depths of the upturned machine when Jade strolled in and perched herself casually on the arm of the sofa.

She watched her mum yank out several yards of carpet thread, then poke a length of wire into various orifices to expel clumps of fluff, sweet wrappers and dog hairs.

Neither of them spoke, but Annie knew her daughter was after something, so she continued her repair job in silence.

By the time Annie got to work with parcel tape on the perished old hose Jade was gritting her teeth and her eyes had glazed over with boredom.

When she could bear it no longer she finally asked,

"If I'm grounded for a fortnight does that mean two Saturdays or three?"

Annie bit the end of the tape with her teeth and ripped a layer of skin off her lip in the process, causing her to swear loudly.

Not a muscle of Jade's face moved as she met her mum's watery eyed stare.

"Why do you ask" Annie said at last.

"Daniel's asked me to go to the pictures with him" said her daughter.

Annie had reached the final stage of the procedure so all that was left to do was wrap an industrial strength elastic band round the catch to keep the lid shut then she sat back in triumph.

"There you go" she said "good as new."

"Well?" asked Jade.

"What's it worth?"

"Dishes and ironing for a month."

"Done."

Jade heaved a sigh of relief.

"Will you tell dad for me as well?"

"Now you're pushing your luck" said her mum, switching on the hoover to check for suction, then cursing as it caught a loose thread and began to unravel the carpet.

Jade grinned on her way out.

"Keep that up mum and you'll have a nice bedside rug in no time."

Later that evening Annie broke the news to Tom.

"NO" he said firmly "definitely not."

"And why not?"

"Because she's only thirteen."

"That's her age, you wally, that's not a reason."

"She's too young, she's not going and that's final."

Annie knew that Jade was on the other side of the door, holding her breath.

"Look, it's only a film and a burger – no big deal."

"But she's only thirteen" Tom tried again.

"They're going in the afternoon for Pete's sake, she'll be home before seven off the last bus."

"She bloody well won't," Tom announced fiercely "I'll go and fetch her myself."

Annie heard the strangled moan from the kitchen, but Tom was still talking.

"And I want to meet this boy first as well."

"Don't be such an old-fashioned fart."

Tom knew he was beaten but, as Annie left the room, she heard him muttering sadly,

"She's still only thirteen."

In the kitchen Jade gave her a quick hug.

"Thanks mum, you're a star."

"Damn right I am," replied Annie "but no doubt you'll have forgotten that by morning."

CHAPTER FIVE

Annie and Aunt Lizzie were in the supermarket, having a fairly heated debate about the old lady's forthcoming birthday which she was insisting should pass by as just another day.

"But it's your 70th" protested Annie "we should do something a bit special."

"Rubbish" said her aunt "I don't want a fuss made, you can take me to the pub for a couple of port and lemons but that's all – and definitely no balloons."

"What about letting us take you out for a meal then?" Annie suggested.

"No need to go to all that expense" said Aunt Lizzie "and by the time everyone says they want to come it will have grown out of all proportion, as usual."

Annie was running out of options.

"Well, how about you choose one of your favourite meals and we'll have that at home, just the family?"

"OK, bangers and mash it is then" the older woman grinned, then marched off with a trolley to do her own shopping.

Annie shook her head in exasperation then wandered off in the other direction, but after perusing a couple of the aisles she came up with an idea – based on stories her mum had told her from the 70's, when Aunt Lizzie used to enjoy cooking a lot and was quite famous for hosting very 'trendy' dinner parties.

After Annie had filled her trolley, keeping a wary eye out for her aunt, she went through the checkout, loaded the shopping into her car then went in search of Lizzie.

It wasn't until she got to the toiletries aisle that Annie finally found her, staring helplessly at the hair products selection.

"What's the problem?" asked Annie.

"I can't find a decent shampoo" the old lady complained.

Annie's gaze travelled over the many shelves full of every combination of hair care she could imagine.

"Are you kidding me," she exclaimed "there must be hundreds to choose from here."

"I can see that, but they're all stupid names and full of weird ingredients I've never heard of, what's wrong with a good old-fashioned medicated shampoo?"

Annie grabbed a bottle and shoved it under Aunt Lizzie's nose.

"Here, strawberry and vanilla – you'll have heard of them, surely?"

The old lady looked scathingly at the bottle, then back at her niece.

"I just want to wash my hair with it, not pour it over bloody ice-cream" she retorted, before stomping off to the checkout.

That Friday, as soon as Jade came in from school, the sitting room was transformed into a beauty parlour for a couple of hours.

Kate was also there, and the plan was that they would all have a pampering session and a make-over, before taking Aunt Lizzie to the pub on the eve of her birthday.

"Not sure if I fancy this," the old lady said warily, when she saw the array of face masks, hot wax strips, tweezers, curling tongs and a variety of other implements that Jade was laying out before them "they look like instruments of torture to me."

"Not to worry," said Jade "most of it's for mum anyway, she needs the most work done."

Annie was quite indignant.

"Bloody cheek" she exclaimed "I'll just have a face mask anyway, don't need a makeover."

Jade snorted in derision.

"Lucky for you we've only got two hours – yours would be a scaffolding job if I was doing it properly."

Then she slipped a headband over Annie's hair, pushed her flat on the sofa and started slapping a mud mask on.

"And you're not allowed to talk while this is on," she instructed, smirking "otherwise it will crack and you'll look like something from a horror movie."

"How will we know the difference?" sniggered Aunt Lizzie.

When they got to the pub it was still quite early and the pool room was empty, so they lay down a row of coins, put a few tunes on the juke box and started playing doubles.

Jade was paired with Aunt Lizzie and the two of them were on top form, winning the first three games in a row, much to the two sister's annoyance.

"We're getting trounced here" Kate moaned "how could you have missed that last shot?"

"Because my eyes are still watering from that bloody waxing" huffed Annie.

Her daughter grinned maliciously.

"Well mum," she retorted "we had to do *something* about your mono-brow."

Her mum glared back at her.

"Bit sneaky waiting till I dozed off though" she complained.

"It would have taken the three of us to hold you down if you'd been awake" her sister pointed out "and it's just as well Tom had taken the boys for a walk so they weren't there to hear you swearing at the end."

After a few more games, where Annie and Kate finally managed to draw level, they played the decider which was narrowly won by Jade and Aunt Lizzie. By this time the room was beginning to fill up with some of the younger locals, so they conceded the table and went through to the bar. The three older women were on their fourth round of drinks and Aunt Lizzie was feeling decidedly mellow.

They had joined a table of four other women they knew who were also on a girls night out so the atmosphere was very merry, even Jade appeared to be enjoying herself and at one point she nudged Aunt Lizzie and said,

"There's a man over there eyeing you up, you know."

They all turned to stare at the person in question who was propped up against the bar, obviously a few sheets to the wind, but when he saw them looking he raised his glass and gave Aunt Lizzie a cheerful, leery wink.

"That's our coalman isn't it" said Annie "you'd hardly recognise him now he's all scrubbed up."

"I think you've pulled, Aunt Lizzie," Kate laughed "shall we invite him over?"

"Don't you dare" the old lady said in a horrified voice "he's wearing a cravat and wellies for heaven's sake."

The rest of the evening went by quickly and they were all enjoying themselves, especially at Aunt Lizzie's expense as her new admirer continued to wink and smile whenever he caught her eye, much to her embarrassment.

She was therefore quite relieved when Tom arrived to take them all home but just as they were gathering up their coats and bags, the man suddenly appeared at their table and announced, slurring,

"I would very much like to ask this lady if she would allow me the pleasure of escorting her home."

Quick as a flash Annie replied,

"You're on mate, drop us off a couple of bags of nutty slack next week and she's all yours."

The next evening Aunt Lizzie, having eventually forgiven Annie for trying to give her away so cheaply, claiming that she was worth a hundredweight of coal at least, was in raptures when her niece served up her 70's theme three course meal. The starter was prawn cocktail, followed by chicken Kiev and then Black Forest gateau for dessert, and she was further delighted when she opened the present Annie had saved till after dinner to discover a years supply of Vosene.

CHAPTER SIX

On the morning of Jade's big date Annie was sitting in the study when a fleeting shadow passed the window for the third time in as many minutes.

Lee had asked if he could have his pal Mark over for the day, Annie wasn't too keen on the boy because he was a bit of a know-all but had agreed anyway, since Lee's grounding was now over as well.

True to form Mark had announced within half an hour of arriving that he was going to teach Sophie to walk on a lead and, even though Lee had tried to explain the futility of it, Mark thought he knew better.

With his vast experience of owning a gerbil and two goldfish the boy was adamant that he could accomplish in one morning what the rest of them had failed to do in six years.

Hence the fleeting shadow.

When Annie finally went outside Mark was on his fourth lap of the house, hanging on to the dog's lead for dear life. His eyes were bulging and his strides were getting increasingly longer as Sophie warmed up to the game and ran faster and faster.

Annie guessed that the boy was now terrified to let go of the lead in case he was launched into orbit, so on their next appearance she stepped into their path and barked full into the dog's face.

The result was spectacular, as Sophie appeared to have an immediate cardiac arrest and collapsed on the spot, while Mark was catapulted on to the grass and lay there winded for a few minutes.

Lee sauntered over to check if the dog was still breathing, gave his pal a withering stare and went indoors for a drink.

"Maybe I'll just try throwing her a stick for now" Mark gasped eventually.

Annie looked down at his smouldering trainers and agreed that was probably best.

Aunt Lizzie had been watching the proceedings from her armchair and as Annie passed she peered over the top of her glasses and whispered,

"There's another one whose lift doesn't go to the top floor, I reckon."

When Kate called in for a coffee Annie was in the kitchen ironing, the sight of which caused her sister's eyebrows to disappear into her hairline. It was common knowledge that this particular chore was top of Annie's hate list.

"I'm only running over a shirt for Jade," Annie said defensively "She's been so long in the bathroom she won't have time."

Kate made no comment, even when her sister continued to work her way through the pile, but watched in fascination as each item was thrown onto the board, battered to a reasonably smooth finish, then whisked on to a hanger.

"So, what's this boy like then?" she asked at last

"He's got a nice bum apparently."

"That's always a good start."

"Tight as two hard boiled eggs in a hankie was how Jade described it."

"Shame he's not coming here to pick her up then."

As she spoke the creaky old ironing board gave up the ghost and collapsed with a crash. Annie was positively euphoric

"Best bloody thing that's happened to me all week" she said, as she picked up the remaining ironing and went to stuff it back in the airing cupboard.

When Jade finally appeared she was wearing combat trousers, one of Tom's checked shirts, unbuttoned and tied at the waist over a little vest top, and a pair of Doc Marten boots. Her hair had been allowed to dry without brushing and was tied loosely on top of her head so that bits of it escaped here and there.

"How do I look?" she asked of the two women.

"Pretty damn good" said Annie.

Tom had been hovering in the background and looked completely bemused.

As Jade and her mum went out of the back door he turned to Kate,

"Two hours she was in that bathroom – two bloody hours" he said.

"I think she looks brilliant" said Kate "you have to spend ages to look as if you haven't tried, that's how it is these days."

"Well, the clothes look OK I suppose" conceded Tom, trying to appear knowledgeable "but what happened from the neck up?"

Outside Annie slipped her daughter an extra tenner and told her to enjoy herself.

"Ta, ma" said Jade "and you will make sure dad stays here today, won't you?"

"Don't you worry" Annie assured her "I've got a chore list as long as my arm – and a rather cunning plan."

As Jade turned to walk up the lane for her bus Annie couldn't resist a parting shot,

"Having said that of course, you'd better keep an eye out in the cinema for anyone lurking nearby wearing dark glasses and a false beard."

"Not funny mum, not funny at all."

"You're right I suppose" agreed Annie "with your dad's luck he'd probably get himself arrested."

After Tom had hammered a few nails into the ironing board, and to be absolutely sure he couldn't escape, Annie asked him to mow the lawn.

As this was roughly the size of a cricket pitch the task usually took at least half a day.

"One of these days I'm going to get myself a sit-upon mower" he moaned, as he hauled at the starter and the old machine coughed and spluttered into life, sending a dense cloud of smoke into his face and causing him to choke for a few minutes.

"You'd think after all these years he'd learn to get his head out of the bloody way in time, wouldn't you?" Aunt Lizzie remarked as he trundled off across the grass.

"I think it's just part of his ritual" said Annie "it wouldn't do to make it look too easy."

After a few lengths of the lawn Tom began to sneeze.

"Bloody hay fever" he said as he passed them again, eyes streaming.

Annie offered no sympathy but fetched him a can of lager instead.

"It's a bit early for that" Aunt Lizzie commented disapprovingly "he'll never get the job done if he's sloshed."

"Oh, I have my reasons" said Annie, mysteriously.

After a few more lengths Tom was still sneezing violently, and for greater effect he crawled past them on his knees, still mowing.

"Give it here, you wally" his wife finally said "I'll have a go for a while."

Tom relinquished control willingly and went indoors for a shower.

By the time he returned Grandad had arrived and between him, Annie and Aunt Lizzie, who was determined not to be left out, the grass was cut in record time.

Tom sat in the sun and enjoyed a few more lagers, giving himself a mental pat on the back at his own cunning and theatrics.

Later on, when Jade phoned to say they'd missed the last bus, Tom was triumphant.

"I knew it – I bloody well knew it" he proclaimed "I told you I should have arranged to pick them up."

"Well, *you* can't go now" Annie pointed out "you've been drinking."

That was the moment Tom realised he'd been had, but that he'd never be able to prove it.

After Annie had dropped Daniel home, she asked Jade how things had gone.

"Not bad" was her daughter's expansive reply "not bad at all."

"Sounds positive enough" said Annie "you were right about his bum too, by the way."

Jade sighed and shook her head very slowly,

"You're not really a normal mum are you" she said.

"That's the nicest thing you've said to me in ages" said Annie.

As soon as they got back Tom pounced.

"Well, what was he like, did you enjoy the film and are you seeing him again?"

Jade looked at her dad as though he'd just dropped in from another planet.

"Which question do you want me to answer first?" was her sarcastic response.

"The main one is did he try anything on?" her dad asked warily.

"Well, yes, he did actually . . . ." Jade started to reply, whereupon Tom did a fantastic impression of a whale bursting through the surface of the ocean as he leapt to his feet and towered over his daughter.

"He did WHAT?" he bellowed.

Jade's baffled gaze swung between her parents as she spoke again,

"He said that since he'd bought the tickets maybe I should pay for the popcorn" she answered indignantly "I told him he was lucky to have me there at all, but that I'd brought stuff anyway – I wasn't going to pay the silly prices the cinema charges."

Tom sank slowly beneath the waves again, letting out a long, slow breath of relief as he sat down heavily, while Annie stepped in to suggest that Jade got herself some supper and her daughter was out of the room before she'd finished the sentence.

"OK" asked her husband "what did *you* think of him?"

"Oh, he was definitely worth your shaving your armpits for" replied Annie.

CHAPTER SEVEN

The weekend of the christening arrived and by ten o' clock on the Saturday morning Annie was sitting on her bench in the garden, completely knackered.

She had put gardening and writing on hold for the past week to get the house in order, as not only were Tom's mum and aunt coming to stay, but also because the christening buffet was being held there as well.

The house was now spotless, the lawn freshly mown and there wasn't a dollop to be seen for miles.

Even Rory, who had an instinct like radar for finding Sophie's deposits, had waddled around for half an hour with his little spade twitching like a divining rod and come back looking disappointed.

Just as she was giving herself a mental pat on the back for a job well done, Annie heard a distant squeal of brakes and looked up to see her mother-in-law's car coming into the lane on two wheels and when it pulled up in the farmyard Aunt Mary was clutching the dashboard with white knuckles and had an even whiter complexion.

It was a well-known fact that Annie's mother-in-law, Ellen, drove as if she were on a Formula One racetrack, especially on motorways, and she always had trouble adjusting her speed when she got to the winding country lanes.

"I nearly missed that turning again" said Ellen as they all trooped into the kitchen "you need a bigger sign at your road end."

Annie thought it best not to point out that since Ellen's last visit the sign had doubled in size and that only an hour ago, she had walked up the lane and tied a huge bunch of balloons to it.

After Tom and Lee had helped to unload the car everyone gathered in the garden for cups of tea and cold drinks. As the day was already heating up the paddling pool had been filled again and they all sat in a circle cooling their feet, while Jade and Lee kept Rory amused at a distance, playing with water pistols.

Ellen and her sister Mary had enjoyed the journey up as they both liked travelling and exploring new places, so much so that most weekends would find them in a different town or village within a thirty-mile radius of their home, searching out the local markets and antique shops.

The two women shared a house in London and Tom and Annie had actually lived with them as well for several months, before their move to Scotland. They still had fond memories of some of the hilarious times they'd had then, stories that were often retold at family gatherings even to this day.

After chatting for an hour or so and getting up to date on family news and the arrangements for the christening, Jade beat Aunt Lizzie to the kitchen to prepare several plates of very normal sandwiches for lunch. Soon after that Ellen announced that she and Mary were going to take a drive into town to check out the antique shops.

Although this was a favourite pastime for both of them, it was one at which Mary had infinitely more success than her sister.

As the two ladies prepared to leave Tom remarked,

"Don't be buying anything until Mary's checked it over for you, will you mum?"

His mother looked offended,

"I don't know what you mean" she sniffed "I thought that kiddies tent I found in the charity shop and sent you last month was a real bargain, even if it didn't have the pegs to go with it."

"Why would it" her son replied, "it was a shower curtain."

The afternoon was spent doing nothing.

The reason being that Annie had forbidden them to have friends for the day in case of any mess they might make, so apart from the paddling pool and garden toys there was no entertainment allowed.

Any food that was consumed had to be eaten outside and from paper plates and cups, then they all had to do a final search of the garden armed with carrier bags for picking up any stray rubbish. By the time the two women returned from town everyone was so bored they were happy to gather round and inspect the new purchases.

Mary had managed to find two more specialised ornaments to add to her collection and an antique silver ring that was much admired.

When it was her turn Ellen produced a brown paper bag,

"Well, I didn't get anything in the antique shops but there was a great little market and I got a real bargain there" she announced, opening the bag "*two* pairs of beach shoes for a fiver."

She pulled her purchases out with a flourish, like a magician producing a rabbit from a hat, and not a word was said when she removed the elastic band from the first pair to discover they were both left feet. The silence continued when the second pair turned out to be two different sizes.

Mary tried hard not to look smug, but Ellen hadn't finished yet,

"Never mind" she said brightly, bringing out another bag "you'll like this one, I bought you a new doorbell."

Tom was surprised at the practicality of the present and was just about to thank her when she continued,

"It plays thirty-two different tunes and I even remembered to buy a battery for it."

The look of horror exchanged by Tom and Annie went unnoticed when Aunt Lizzie suddenly pointed to Rory who was waddling unsteadily down the path, spade in hand and heading straight for where Grandad was weeding the flower bed.

Then they realised what was on the spade and Tom sprinted across the grass but was just too late to prevent his son from tipping its contents into Grandad's cup of tea.

Tom grabbed Rory, the spade and the mug and made a break for the kitchen, leaving the old man staring after them, completely speechless.

The following day, after the christening was over, everyone gathered back at the house for the buffet. Annie was pleased that things had gone fairly smoothly, apart from the moment when Rory had given the lady minister a slap when she'd sprinkled water on his head.

Despite this assault, Christine had cheerfully accepted their invitation to join them and was now sitting talking to Grandad, who had his hearing aid on at full volume especially for the occasion. He was unaware that Annie had removed the battery in case the whistling should drown out the ceremony in church.

There were a number of older children, and they were out in the garden being entertained by Uncle Joe, Annie and Kate's brother. Joe lived some distance away but came to visit quite regularly, and always when there was a special occasion. He was an ex-military bandsman as well so at this moment he had all the children marching in time, up and down the lawn and banging on various makeshift drums, making as much noise as they liked. The only condition was that they did not let Sophie into the house under any circumstances, and Cinders had vanished the moment she saw them all return, so there was no danger of her attacking any of the guests.

It was all going so smoothly in fact that Annie began to feel uneasy.

After circling for a while she signalled to Tom to rescue Christine, who had been cuddling Amy for a while, but now had Rory on her lap and was being force fed soggy cucumber sandwiches so his dad took him, protesting loudly, through for his nap.

A few minutes later, just as one of the guests was congratulating Annie and Kate on what a great day it had been, the sitting room door crashed open and Sophie bounded in, closely followed by Lee

"Sorry mum" he gasped "she slipped her collar and we just couldn't catch her."

Annie's gaze was dragged from her son to the dog and she groaned aloud as she recognised Sophie's familiar stance – front legs down, back end high in the air – and pointing straight at the minister.

Annie closed her eyes and offered up a silent prayer,

"Please God, don't let this happen – not to one of your own."

But it did, with a vengeance.

Into the stunned silence of the room Sophie let rip with one of her longest and loudest farts ever.

Annie still had her eyes closed when she heard Lee say cheerfully,

"It's not the noise you have to worry about – just wait till you catch the fall-out."

His last few words were slightly muffled as Tom returned at that moment, grabbed Lee by the shirt collar, Sophie by the scruff of her neck, and frogmarched them both out of the room.

Ellen and Mary went home the following morning, but not before Ellen insisted that Tom fix up the new doorbell.

"You never know" she said with a poker straight face "it might be a dud."

Unfortunately, it worked perfectly, and there were indeed thirty-two tunes because Ellen also insisted on hearing them all, while showing Rory exactly which buttons to press.

When she was satisfied that her revenge for the shower curtain remark was complete Ellen and her sister gave their farewell hugs, waved a cheery goodbye and drove off up the lane.

"It was clever of Nan to think of putting the doorbell that low down, wasn't it" said Lee, through gritted teeth.

And while Rory stood in the front porch, happily pushing the buttons time and time again, the rest of them sneaked out of the back door into the garden.

CHAPTER EIGHT

A week later and with Rory's first birthday approaching, Jade asked Annie what she was doing about his party.

"Nothing" said Annie "he's not having one."

Jade was shocked.

"Mum, that's really mean, you have to have a party for him."

"Look, he'll never know the difference, so what's the point?"

Something suddenly occurred to her daughter,

"Does that mean Lee and I didn't have one either?"

"Can't you remember, dear?"

"No, of course not."

"I rest my case then" said her mum.

"You can be really heartless at times."

"I know, it's a bummer isn't it?"

"I want to do one for him."

"You don't know what you're saying, child."

"I mean it mum, I'll do one."

"You're on your own then."

"Good grief, it's only a few toddlers, how difficult could that be?"

As her daughter went off to write a few lists Annie smirked to herself and considered the idea of having a girly afternoon in the pub on the day in question.

The front door was opened to the strains of "The Star Spangled Banner' and the last two guests were deposited. While their mum beat a hasty retreat down the path, Annie took the twins through to the sitting room to find Jade on her knees with a bucket and cloth.

"It's just a spot of juice" her daughter assured her "no problem at all, mum."

"Right you are then" said Annie and went back to her computer.

Half an hour later the volume had risen to such an extent that she couldn't resist another look.

This time Jade looked decidedly more harassed.

"Ben's been sick behind the sofa" she said.

"He does that a lot" said Annie.

"And I haven't seen Cinders since they were using her as target practise for the sausage rolls, then Adam poked Beth in the eye when she tried to kiss him."

"She does that a lot too."

"So, I'd better clean up the sick then?" Jade tried again.

"Right you are then" said Annie, and left her to it once more.

Another half hour passed before Tom came in.

"She needs help" he said cautiously.

"I know" said Annie, tapping away at her keyboard.

"I'll go and give her a hand then?" he offered.

"No, you won't – she insisted we weren't to interfere."

"You can be really heartless at times, you know."

"So I've been told."

Tom sighed and went back outside to tinker with the lawnmower.

Just before the parents were due to arrive Annie went to survey the damage.

When she entered the room she found two children fighting over the last piece of pizza, Ben had been sick again over a plate of sandwiches and she had to forcibly remove a chocolate finger from up Beth's nose.

Aunt Lizzie, meanwhile, had discovered an angelic looking three year old on the toilet, dismembering a rag doll whilst singing 'Jesus loves the little children' at the pitch of her lungs and Tom eventually came across Sophie hyperventilating in the utility room after having a balloon burst in her face.

Amongst all the chaos Jade sat curled up in an armchair, staring into the middle distance and whimpering quietly to herself.

"Can I rely on you for next year then?" asked her mum

Jade stirred slightly and gazed up at Annie with a haunted expression before saying hoarsely,

"I'd rather stick pins in my eyes."

CHAPTER NINE

The supermarket was fairly quiet as Kate and Annie strolled slowly round, Amy sleeping peacefully in her car seat in one trolley and Rory sitting in the other, munching on a small box of raisins, Adam having been left at home with his dad.

Annie had decided to throw Tom a surprise fortieth birthday party which was less than a month away so they were shopping for that and Kate would take it home to store in her freezer.

"So, have you worked out final numbers yet?" asked Kate.

"I'm still adding to my list but it's up to about fifty so far."

"Does that include kids?"

"Hell no, I'm hoping to get rid of my three for the night as well, if I can."

"Couldn't we just shove them all upstairs and pay Jade to look after them?"

"She's still having trouble stringing a sentence together after Rory's little do last week."

"Fair enough" said Kate "no kids it is then."

They continued to shop and chat more about the party arrangements until they turned the corner of the next aisle and Annie's trolley jack-knifed into a six-foot display of cornflakes.

By the time she'd apologised and helped the young assistant to pick up a few boxes Kate was nowhere to be seen.

Annie caught up with her sister in an adjoining checkout and had the satisfaction of watching her dive in all directions to catch her shopping as the cashier hurled it through the scanner at the speed of light, while she herself had managed to get one with a trainee staff member who helped pack her bags.

Just as the last item was tucked away safely there was a loud continuous bleep behind her and Annie turned to see Rory sitting in the cashier's lap.

"This item doesn't appear to have a bar code" the woman said drily.

A few days later Annie waited till Tom had left for work then spent the morning on the phone issuing verbal invitations for his party.

After several hours she had confirmed fifty guests, all but one couple coming without children.

Tom's sister, Linda was delighted with the invitation. She and her husband Phil had been part of Tom and Annie's social circle before they'd moved to Scotland and they'd shared many an alcohol-fueled evening together. They also had three children, all close in age to Jade and Lee, so Annie decided not to bother getting rid of hers for the night as they'd be company for each other.

"It's your fault I can't leave the kids behind anyway" Linda pointed out "since you've invited mum and Aunt Mary, I've got no babysitters left down here."

"Not to worry," Annie replied "I'll make an exception for you since you're coming all the way from London, and you can bring that mutt of yours as well, Sophie will be happy then too".

"I could always try and lose them in one of the motorway services on the way up, how does that sound?"

"No, let them come" said Annie "they'll be handy for waiting on people."

She put the phone down and started writing a few more lists then realised it was past Rory's lunchtime when she saw him with his hand in the bag of dried dog food, so she lifted him into his highchair and strapped him in.

When he'd finished eating Annie wiped the spaghetti and semolina off Rory, the walls and the dog and was about to take him through for his nap when the phone rang again.

"Hello, is that the lady mud wrestler?" asked the voice at the other end.

Annie sighed and immediately held Lee responsible for this one.

However, it turned out that the caller had phoned the previous day and a very nice 'older lady' had assured him he had the right number, but the person he wanted wasn't there at the time and to phone again today.

"She told me you did it for charity" said the man.

It took Annie quite some time to convince him that she was not now, nor ever had been, 'Fanny the Amazon' before she finally hung up.

When Aunt Lizzie returned from the village it took her the best part of an hour to rewind the ball of wool that Annie had tied to the leg of her bed then wound round every stick of furniture in her room.

Two weeks before the party Annie was at the top of a ladder hanging wallpaper when Jade wandered in.

"I need a new pair of trainers" she announced.

Her mum continued to smooth down the paper with an old terry nappy and said nothing.

"I could pay a bit towards them" Jade tried again "I've got some birthday money left."

"How much do you have, exactly?"

"Probably a tenner."

"And how much are the trainers, pray tell?"

"About sixty quid."

The ladder wobbled dangerously as Annie turned to throw the nappy at her daughter, but Jade was already gone, so it landed on Sophie instead.

The cloth hung over the dog's head like a judge's wig as she gazed up at Annie sadly.

"Don't you look at me like that" said Annie "she's not getting them and that's final."

As the day drew nearer the family began to feel the sharp edge of Annie's tongue because the tension of trying to keep it secret was getting to her, and she was having a hard time finding excuses to explain her sudden apparent interest in decorating and housework.

However, two days beforehand she began to relax a little, so much so that when Tom fell out of the loft and landed upright in the laundry bin, she was full of concern for him.

Her husband was quite touched at the fuss she made of him, unaware that she'd had a good old snigger about it with Kate later that same day.

"The silly bugger smashed straight through the lid" she laughed "I had visions of him at the party with his leg in plaster but fortunately he only took the skin off his shins."

The day before the big event Lee searched his sister out in the garden.

"I reckon now would be a good time to ask mum about your trainers again" he said.

"How come" asked Jade.

"Because I've just seen her singing along to her party tapes and she's ironing a duster."

They sat in awed silence for a moment and Jade considered writing this in her diary.

CHAPTER TEN

The Saturday of Tom's birthday finally dawned, and it was a scorcher.

Annie fixed him a big fried breakfast then she and the children took it to him in bed.

He was astounded when Annie dragged a huge cardboard box into the room but tried not to look too disappointed when he opened it to find a new ironing board and laundry bin.

However, he was greatly chuffed on discovering his new golf bag, gloves and golf balls downstairs, so when Kate's husband Sam arrived soon after to take him out for the day, he still didn't suspect a thing.

Sam had been primed that he was to keep Tom out of the way until seven that evening.

"Whatever happens, *don't* bring him home too early" his wife had warned him "even if you have to injure yourself and spend a few hours in A&E to pass the time."

As soon as their car disappeared the action began.

Kate arrived with a car boot full of food while their brother Joe, who had stayed in the local pub the night before, brought the drink and a huge music system. Jade and Lee were consigned to Annie's study with hundreds of balloons and a couple of pumps.

Just before lunch Tom's sister Linda and her family arrived, tooting all the way down the lane with the strains of "Bohemian Rhapsody" blasting from the open windows.

As they all piled out and their collie Beth ran to find her pal Sophie, fourteen-year old Nick was heard to announce,

"Excellent journey – Sarah puked twice, Beth piddled in Jack's shoes and mum got stopped for speeding."

His dad, Phil, rolled his eyes and shrugged,

"Just about what you'd expect from this family, so no surprises there really."

The afternoon was riotous as they erected a large marquee and strung miles of lights up between the trees that surrounded the garden, helped along by a few glasses of cider or beer to quench everyone's thirst.

Another dozen or so guests arrived mid-afternoon to help out, as well as pitch their own tents along the far end of the lawn so that it soon resembled a small campsite, so much so that they even had to convince a minibus full of German tourists who drove down the lane that this was not the case. On closer inspection they seemed quite relieved to have been mistaken and went hurriedly on their way.

Ellen and Mary arrived at four, called a halt to the alcohol consumption for a spell and made a mountain of sandwiches and huge pots of coffee – by six thirty there was nothing to do but wait.

On the stroke of seven Sam's car came down the lane and when the two men got out of the car a few dozen party poppers were released, someone opened champagne and the party was officially started.

Tom was absolutely delighted at the sight of so many friends and family members and got right into the swing of things immediately. One of his specialties at parties was to introduce mad games that suited all ages, so the children were having as much fun as the adults, and as the evening wore on the games got more and more ridiculous.

All but one of the guests was having a ball.

The exception was a woman called Nancy who they didn't know all that well but who was a bit of a snob and spent the entire time looking down her nose at the proceedings and refusing to join in. The only reason she'd been invited was that her husband was the complete opposite – Harry was a good friend of Tom's, as well as a work colleague, with a great sense of humour and was liked by all of them, so Annie had decided that they could put up with Nancy for a few hours, rather than not having Harry there at all.

Throughout the evening Nancy had avoided all the fun, spent most of it nursing a glass of soda water and definitely did not approve of the fact that her husband was not only participating in most of the games but was also thoroughly enjoying them.

To begin with Harry had kept her company and tried to persuade her to let her hair down and join in but eventually realised he was wasting his time, so after a couple of hours he just left her to it and kept disappearing to the bar whenever he had the chance.

Some time later Nancy was sitting at the kitchen table and bent down to pick up a stray cocktail sausage just as Sophie strolled past and, right on cue, farted so badly that it cleared the room for ten minutes, leaving Nancy gasping for air.

"Pity Harry missed that," Tom said on a hiccup "but he's heaving his heart out behind the hydrangeas at the moment."

Annie was impressed that her husband had even thought that sentence up, let alone said it and made himself understood.

By eleven o'clock Nancy was becoming increasingly annoyed at the fact that her husband seemed to have done a disappearing act, but everyone's lips were sealed as to his whereabouts.

One of their more energetic games outside had involved a pack of cards, a circle of chairs and a lot of changing of seats until very often there were as many as six people sitting on one unfortunate person's lap. When it was over Harry had been found at the bottom of one such pile, almost unconscious, so Tom and Sam had hidden him behind Annie's desk in the study, complete with a bucket.

It only added to Nancy's horror that the games continued to get even more ridiculous, involving matchboxes, fancy dress clothes and brooms and when someone suggested that she should shove a banana into her cleavage she nearly had an attack of the vapours.

If she could have laid hands on Harry at that moment she would have wiped the floor with him, because the only thing that was keeping her there was the fact that Harry had the car and house keys, and still no-one was prepared to give away his hiding place.

By 1am there were a few casualties sprawled around the garden, asleep where they lay, but Annie was enjoying herself far too much to worry about a few mangled marrows and crushed cauliflowers.

Some of the tents looked as if they'd had a party of their own where people had tripped over guys ropes, causing them to sag drunkenly or collapse altogether. Even the knackered old caravan was tipped at a crazy angle because Annie had forgotten to lower the stabilisers when they'd repositioned it that afternoon.

The remaining guests' dancing abilities had deteriorated gradually throughout the night and the few couples who were attempting romantic slow dances were only doing so in an effort to keep each other upright.

Annie, Kate and Linda were having the time of their lives and hadn't even bothered asking their husbands to dance.

They knew this would have been futile because, not only were the men completely devoid of rhythm, but they'd taken root by the bar and not even dynamite would shift them.

Linda's sixteen-year old son Jack had enjoyed the attention of several young teenage girls during the evening and his dad, Phil, watched him proudly from a distance.

"That's my boy" he said drunkenly "even having his parents here hasn't cramped his style."

Linda overheard this as she appeared behind him and helped herself to another drink.

In one lightning move she pulled out the front of Phil's trousers and dropped a handful of ice cubes in.

"Bet that'll cramp your style for a bit though" she said, before weaving her way across the grass to rejoin the others.

When three o'clock came things were finally winding down and anyone who was still conscious had gathered in the kitchen.

Nancy was now almost weeping with frustration and had refused Annie's invitation to grab a duvet and get her head down behind the sofa. She sat glaring at everyone and ignored any attempt to draw her into conversation, even when Phil had given her a hearty slap on the back and offered to give her a piggy-back round the garden.

Tom was propped up against the fridge, trying to keep Phil's face in focus while they debated which of their wives was the daftest.

Just as they finally agreed that the two women were equally insane the door opened and Harry staggered in.

There was a united and very audible intake of breath followed by a moment of frozen silence as Nancy looked daggers at Harry and he peered sleepily back at her – then some joker started to whistle the theme tune from 'The Good, the Bad and the Ugly' and all hell broke loose.

Nancy tried to stand up, only to find herself pinned down by Sam's very firm hand on her shoulder as she yelled at her husband to give her the damned keys, while at the same time Harry took a step backward and fell against the tumble drier, clicking the door shut.

As the machine started to rotate, he was pushed roughly aside by Tom, who shouted,

"Mind the bloody cat" and hauled the drier door open

After a split second a spitting, snarling projectile shot out of the depths of the drier like a heat-seeking missile – and its target was Nancy.

Cinders landed in her lap with claws out and ready for the kill and there was complete bedlam for several minutes as Nancy screamed while Tom and Sam tried to prise them apart and Harry slid slowly down the wall to land in a crumpled heap on the floor.

When the uproar finally died down Cinders was evicted and Kate led Nancy away to the study to recover.

Then Tom went to help Harry get up and discovered he was having quiet but uncontrollable hysterics.

He eventually got to his feet and as he was guided away in the opposite direction to his wife he paused for a moment by Annie's chair and whispered,

"I want that cat – just name your price."

The scene at breakfast time was very subdued as people sat round the table comparing hangovers and refusing Annie's offers of left-over curry or a fry up.

The tale of Nancy and Cinders was related to those who hadn't witnessed it and caused several people to hold their heads in agony while they laughed.

Tom had finally retrieved the keys for Nancy and she had burnt rubber all the way up the lane.

Just as the story was coming to an end Harry breezed in, looking as fresh as a daisy and announced that he was starving. He cooked his own fry-up, chatting all the while but with no mention of his wife, then went to sit in the garden to eat.

Cinders sat by his side on the bench and gazed up at him adoringly as he fed her bits of bacon but when Tom saw them out of the window he couldn't help thinking of condemned men and hearty breakfasts.

CHAPTER ELEVEN

Since the London crowd didn't have to go home until the Monday, it was decided that the best way to use up all the leftover food and drink was to have another small party.

This time, however, it would take place by the river that ran down past the farmyard and would only begin when the house and garden were put back in order.

Annie was in her element because they had so many helpers that she could rush around waving her chore lists and appear to be frantically busy, whilst actually managing to do very little.

Her only concern was re-erecting the canes for the runner beans and straightening the pea fences which had suffered minor damage from wandering, inebriated guests the night before.

By mid afternoon it was all more or less back to normal so between them they ferried the necessary provisions across the yard and down to the river bank.

Even Aunt Lizzie's armchair went, much to Grandad's disgust.

"That daft old bat will be expecting a carpet and curtains next" he complained.

"And where would I hang the curtains, I ask you?" Aunt Lizzie called across to him.

"She's got ears like a bat as well" Grandad muttered, but cheered up when he saw the second armchair being lifted across for him.

By the time everyone gathered again there were over thirty people, including children. Some of them were the ones who'd camped overnight and a few more brave souls who had phoned to thank them for the party had been delighted to be invited back. There were, of course, a fair number who hadn't the stamina or nerve for another one, all they wanted to do was curl up at home with the hangovers they already had.

The children spent most of the time in the river, some of the adults paddled occasionally and the two dogs divided their time between the water and diving for crusts.

Even Phil, who had a distinct aversion to water, had been persuaded to lie across one of the enormous old inner tubes and just float around in the shallows.

"I'm amazed" said his wife "the only time you'd normally see him near water is sitting on a stool with a fishing rod in one hand and a can of lager in the other."

"Sounds like he'd make a good garden gnome" said Aunt Lizzie.

Ellen and Mary sat on cushions on some large rocks, dangling their feet in the water and with a flask and a pile of sandwiches between them.

"That dog's hopeless" Mary remarked as they watched Sophie try to catch the crusts being thrown at her and Bess.

She would stand poised, like a goalie about to take a penalty, then as the bread was frisbeed through the air she invariably misjudged her move and got it right between the eyes. Bess didn't miss once, and she was also fast enough to nip beneath Sophie and pinch all the ones she'd missed.

The big dog put up with this for a while, but when she'd had enough she just put one massive paw on the smaller dogs back and leaned heavily, until Bess was spread-eagled and yelping for mercy, then Sophie finally let her go.

"That's impressive" Linda commented "has she been taking self-assertion classes"?

"Not at all" said Annie" she's only showing off because Cinders isn't here."

The cat had watched their departure from her branch in the apple tree with such a look of contempt that they knew she was going to make them pay for this weekend for a very long time.

After being suitably squashed Bess took to the river again, swimming close to Phil, who had dozed off and was drifting slowly towards the women on the rocks.

"What *does* that man look like?" Mary asked.

"Like someone with a serious case of piles, I'd say" replied her sister.

Just as she spoke they saw Phil's sandwich drop into the water from his relaxed hand and Bess open her jaws wide to catch it.

The next moment there was an almighty bang, the two women were almost blown off their rocks and Phil disappeared under the water.

When he surfaced he realised it was a good thing he could actually swim because no-one else there would have been capable of saving him.

"Bloody charming" he shouted at them as they all rolled around, helpless with laughter "I thought I'd been shot."

This only made them worse so it was up to him to squelch his way up the riverbank and administer a quick spot of first-aid to Sophie, who appeared to have fainted.

CHAPTER TWELVE

A week later all was more or less back to normal, it was a Saturday and everyone was just doing their own thing, enjoying a quiet morning with no pressure - and no-one chasing after them with a chore list.

Breakfast was over, Annie was in the garden, the two older children lazing in their bedrooms, amusing Rory between them and Tom and Aunt Lizzie were having coffee and a chinwag, sitting at the kitchen table.

For no particular reason they were both in high spirits and having a good laugh at some of the events they remembered from the previous weekend, until the back door crashed open and Annie stormed in.

"Those piggin' birds are at my grass seeds again" she almost shouted, glaring at the pair of them, while they stared back wordlessly, trying to hide their amusement.

At the start of the week Annie had decided to dig over an area of the garden that was unused and neglected and thought it would be easier just to grass it to make it look tidier, ignoring Tom's comment that the last thing he needed was even more lawn to cut.

"And if they're not eating the seeds they're having flamin' dust baths all over it," she continued to moan "it's going to be really patchy when it comes through."

Tom and Aunt Lizzie sat patiently waiting for her tirade to finish.

"The bloody cheek of them" she ranted on "they don't know who they're messing with" then after a slight pause she turned on them accusingly,

"And what were you two tittering about anyway."

Aunt Lizzie couldn't contain herself at that remark and started to laugh out loud.

"Tittering" Tom snorted "did she just say 'tittering'?

The older woman had her hanky out by this time and was wiping her eyes as Tom went on,

"No-one says 'tittering' these days for Pete's sake, haven't heard that in years."

Aunt Lizzie nodded emphatically and managed to croak,

"Well, not since Frankie Howard popped his clogs anyway" which set them both off again.

"I've had enough of this" snapped Annie "I'm going for a cigarette – and I might even have a glass of bloody wine as well, don't care if it is only 11 in the morning."

As she exited into the living room the other two adults looked at each other, grinning, then Lizzie said in an undertone,

"That girl smokes like a chimney," to which Tom replied

"And drinks like a fish"

"Swears like a trooper," sniggered the old lady, then Tom finished by whispering.

"Farts like a horse."
And once again they were helpless.

Annie had stormed into the living room just as Jade came in through the opposite door from the hall.
"Mum, I was going to ask you something......." she began, then caught the look on Annie's face and faltered "but maybe later will do."
At the same time she became aware of the noises from the kitchen.
"Who's making all that racket?" she asked
"That'll be your dad and Aunt Lizzie – 'tittering'," Annie said caustically.
Jade rolled her eyes,
"Mum, if dad's on Twitter I think you probably mean they're tweeting."
"I bloody well know what I mean" Annie roared "and they were very definitely 'tittering', except now they seem to have moved on to guffawing and chortling."
At the sight of her daughters completely blank expression Annie bellowed,
"Good grief child, didn't Enid Blyton teach you anything?"

Later that day Annie had calmed down enough to take a break and was sitting outside, watching Tom and Aunt Lizzie's antics at the other end of the garden with great amusement.
"We felt a bit mean at not taking you seriously earlier" Tom had explained "so we thought we'd have a go at making a scarecrow."

The two of them had been working at it for over an hour and progress was slow.

Tom had supplied a pair of old wellies, some combat trousers, an old sweatshirt and a battered cowboy hat and he and Aunt Lizzie were trying to stuff the shirt and trousers with hay.

Jade, surprisingly, had come out to join her mum and watch the show.

"Wouldn't it make more sense to have tied them at the ends" she asked, as the pair stuffed a trouser leg each and the hay fell through the bottom for the second time.

"That would spoil the fun" laughed Annie "don't you dare suggest it."

Eventually that thought did occur to them though, and after tying the sleeve and trouser ends they kept on packing in the hay while mother and daughter tried to keep straight faces.

"He's getting a bit lopsided" observed Jade "and they should have used a smaller sack for the head, it's too big for the hat now."

When the scarecrow was finally finished he was about eight feet tall, his wellies were pointing in different directions and he had the girth of Desperate Dan. His head was top heavy and the hat kept falling off until Aunt Lizzie sewed it in place with bright red wool and a darning needle, remarking that it looked like 'a pea on a monument'.

"Well, what do you think" asked Tom proudly, as he completed the job by hanging the dummy by the neck from the clothesline.

Annie and Jade had been beside themselves for the past ten minutes, but his wife finally managed to say,

"I'm not sure if he'll *scare* that many birds" she gasped "but they might die laughing."

Ten minutes later Jade took advantage of her mum's good humour, brought her a glass of wine and finally asked,

"Would it be ok if Daniel came over for the afternoon tomorrow?"

Annie paused with the glass halfway to her lips,

"Seriously? You've managed to keep him away from us for months so I can't believe you'd actually consider bringing the poor guy into the lion's den – I thought you liked him?"

Jade's expression was one of bemusement,

"It was his idea really" she admitted "I was telling him about the party and for some bizarre reason he seems to think our family is kind of cool and he'd like to meet you."

Annie looked at her daughter and asked slyly,

"And you don't mind him meeting *all* of us?"

Jade reddened slightly.

"Well, maybe not Lee, not just yet anyway."

"And why would that be, I wonder" asked Annie, enjoying the sight of her daughter's discomfort.

"Oh, mum, you know what he's like – he'd just keep hanging around being a pest" Jade protested "showing off his slug collection or talking about bodily functions and stuff."

Annie allowed the following silence to stretch out as long as possible then Jade spoke again,

"I don't suppose you'd let me lock him in the coal shed for a couple of hours, would you?"

There was a fractional pause as Annie tried to calculate how much kindling could be chopped in that time, then she shook her head,

"I'm pretty sure there are laws against that sort of thing these days" she said "anyway, he might be fine – he's not as immature as you think, you know."

As the words left her lips there was a distant rumbling noise and a moment later Lee hurtled round the corner of the house on his skateboard, wearing a Sumo fat suit and shouting 'GERONIMO' at the top of his voice.

He sailed past them, hit an uneven slab on the path and flew though the air, arms and legs flailing, before belly-flopping into the paddling pool.

Jade turned to look her mum full in the face and spoke quietly, her voice dripping with sarcasm,

"You were saying?"

CHAPTER THIRTEEN

"Haven't they caught that bloody animal yet?" asked Aunt Lizzie "those poor kids are going to be knackered before we even start."

She was peering out of the kitchen window, watching Jade and Lee in their vain attempts to catch Sophie and get a collar on her so that Annie could take her to where she would stay for the week that they were all away on their annual big family holiday.

"Never mind," said their mum "at least they can sleep on the journey."

They had been out there for half an hour already and were no closer to catching her than at the start.

Sophie had been watching them packing for two days now and had been walking around with a pathetic expression because she knew something was up.

She'd watched again that morning as Annie had loaded the boot of her car with the dog bed, blankets, food bowls and chewy toys but when they'd tried to entice her into the car

Sophie had taken off like a rocket and they'd been chasing her ever since.

"Piggin' silly dog would be fine if she knew where she was going" muttered Aunt Lizzie.

Annie was only taking Sophie to the other side of the village to stay with the woman who was responsible for them having her in the first place.

Carol ran a small animal sanctuary where animals of all shapes and sizes had been rescued by her and when she'd heard they were looking for a dog she'd phoned them about Sophie who was just two years old and had been rescued from a negligent owner. That was six years ago and they'd gone to see her, under no obligation, and brought her home with them that same day.

Aunt Lizzie was now staring out of the window that looked onto the farmyard.

"He's not doing very well out there either" she commented.

Tom was standing by the back of his car, surrounded by a mountain of suitcases and other assorted luggage.

"That's the second time he's unloaded everything."

Annie opened the window and leaned out,

"What's the problem?" she called

"The problem is that it's only a family car – not the bloody Tardis" shouted Tom.

Annie shut the window,

"Miserable git" she said.

Just then Lee came to the back door to announce that they'd finally caught the dog and tied her to the climbing frame.

He had barely finished speaking when they heard Jade yell and they looked out to see Sophie loping across the lawn, dragging the frame behind her. She was making for the farmyard but came to a shuddering standstill when she charged through the side gate and the frame wouldn't follow.

Annie untangled her, put her straight in the car and drove off, leaving Jade and Lee stretched out on the lawn, gasping for breath, while Tom unloaded the car yet again.

By the time they'd reached Carol's smallholding Sophie had shown her displeasure by filling the car with noxious fumes so Annie was relieved to get out and take a few deep breaths of fresh air.

She stood there for a few minutes, watching and listening to the clamour of all the different animals and marvelling again at the assortment.

There were rabbits, chickens, whippets, goats and guinea fowl, a couple of ponies, some llamas, a few pigs, countless cats and kittens and at least half a dozen Harlequin Danes that Carol bred and sold in order to finance the rest of them.

Annie often wondered if there was an ark hidden somewhere behind the house but she hadn't spotted it yet.

Carol's husband was the first to greet her and immediately launched into the story of their latest acquisition.

"She went to an auction yesterday, looking for a horse blanket she told me," he explained "then she phoned me to say I might not like the one she'd bought because it came with a head and four legs attached."

He pointed to a flea bitten, lop-eared old donkey who was gazing over the fence at him adoringly, then went over to give it a scratch under the chin and a carrot.

Carol arrived just then and made such a huge fuss of Sophie that the dog simpered like a half wit and all Annie got was one last fart by way of a farewell gesture.

Back home they were almost ready, Kate and her family had arrived with Grandad so while Tom loaded Annie's boot with the remaining luggage, she phoned Ellen and Linda to say they were leaving.

They'd chosen a small seaside town that was roughly the same distance for the London crowd to travel up to as it was for the Scottish clan to drive down and had rented four cottages between them.

All that was left was to lock up and leave the key out for Harry, who had offered to feed Cinders and the rabbit in their absence.

"It's a wonder he didn't just stay here for the week," said Aunt Lizzie "he'd probably get more conversation out of the cat than he does Nancy these days."

"You're probably right" agreed Annie, as they drove away with Cinders sneering down at them from her tree "and that animal will be hell to live with by the time he's spoilt her rotten for a week"

"I wouldn't put it past her to have the place booby trapped when we get back" her aunt remarked.

CHAPTER FOURTEEN

It was mid-afternoon by the time the entire gang met up at the beach huts they'd hired, it had been agreed that this would be their first stop to unload all the larger items before going to the cottages.

As they plodded to and fro with folding chairs, windbreaks, dinghies, fishing tackle, a camping stove, kettle, pots and pans, other families on the beach watched them with great amusement.

"This is embarrassing," moaned Phil, after his third trip from the cars "I expect there'll be a chemical toilet to unload next."

"Cheer up, you miserable sod," said Linda "you're on holiday."

"I see you managed to lose the old goat on the way" Aunt Lizzie remarked to Kate, referring to Grandad's absence.

"Unfortunately not," said Kate "he was getting grumpy and wanted to stretch his legs so I pointed out the cottage to him and he's meeting us there in an hour."

When everything was finally unloaded they locked the huts and made their way to the cottages. There the men were left to unpack the rest of the luggage and mind the children while the women headed for the only supermarket in the small town.

On entering the shop Ellen, Mary and Lizzie took a trolley each for food, while the other three grabbed one between them and headed straight for the drinks aisle.

As they approached it Linda murmured,

"Don't look now but isn't that your dad, hovering by the Guinness pyramid?"

"That'll be him alright" said Kate.

When they reached him the old man looked smug,

"Couldn't find the damned cottage again but I knew if I waited here long enough you'd turn up – you bunch of drunks."

They looked into his trolley, containing a large box of teabags, a giant pack of loo rolls, two crates of beer, several bottles of wine and a bottle of spiced rum then they looked at each other and said nothing.

The following morning everyone met on the beach and set up camp. The plan was that they would all come and go throughout the day as long as there were at least two adults left to keep an eye on their belongings.

One of the dinghies was filled with water for Rory, Adam and Amy to splash about in and to begin with everyone was happy to laze around for an hour or so, especially the men, who had celebrated their first night a little too well.

They were seriously hung over and complaining to each other about their wives warped sense of humour,

"That bloody daftie of mine rolled up the legs on all of my trousers when she packed" Phil complained.

"I've got knots in the corners of all my hankies" countered Tom.

They looked expectantly at Sam, who raised his foot in the air and wiggled his toes,

"She's hidden my trainers and I've got seven brand new pairs of flip flops, all in different colours."

After lunch Mary and Ellen went for a stroll round the town to check out the market and antique shops and at the same time keep an eye out for Grandad who had announced that morning after just half an hour on the beach,

"The sun's too hot, the water's too cold and there's too much bloody sand altogether, I'm off for a walk."

The older children also went exploring the town for a while and they came back first to report that they'd spotted him in the amusement arcade, hogging a one-armed bandit. He'd given them all some money and told them to bugger off and stop distracting him.

Throughout the afternoon more reports on him filtered back to the beach.

His daughters had spotted him in the distance, tucking into cockles and candy floss, Ellen and Mary saw him in the bingo hall and when the men went for a quick 'hair of the dog' they found him perched on a bar stool, surrounded by cuddly toys and chatting up the barmaid.

By the time they all got back to their cottages at teatime he was sound asleep on the sofa, clutching his prizes and snoring fit to suck the wallpaper off.

The next couple of days passed in a similar vein but by mid-week they'd decided to have a day out, take in some local scenery and try a different beach.

"Not much of a change," moaned Aunt Lizzie "same sea, different sand."

"Well the shops will be different" said Ellen.

"No they won't, they all sell the same old tat, it's only the postcards that have a different name on them."

"You can stay here then, you miserable old bat" said Grandad.

"Bloody charming" she said, going off in the huff with her knitting.

"We can't go anywhere till the men get back from fishing anyway," said Ellen "I need to wash my car windows anyway, can't see out of them for seagull droppings."

"More like a bloody albatross from the look of it" Grandad muttered, as he too went off to find something to do.

When only the three mums were left they made a start on the picnic.

Their husbands had all been out since 5am, very hungover but determined to get some fish.

"If they catch anything at all it will be a miracle," said Kate "Sam couldn't even get his socks on without falling over."

"Tom's the same, he put two different shoes on and didn't even notice."

"Well, I reckon Phil would have been asleep again before he even dangled his rod."

There was a slight pause before Kate said,

"I think you'll find there's a cure for that these days."

Shortly afterwards the men arrived home triumphant at have caught a couple of small sea trout.

"See, I told you we'd get something" Phil said proudly.

The women looked at the meagre catch without enthusiasm.

"How far do you think that lot will go round eighteen of us?" Linda asked grumpily.

"I'm not sure" Phil responded, grinning "but if you nip out and get five loaves I'll see what I can do."

"Very funny" said his wife "now get this lot cleared up and take that disgusting bait out of my kitchen."

"Not till we've had some breakfast first" said Tom "we're starving."

The women went through to the sitting room and decided to have a drink.

"Well, it is mid-morning" Annie pointed out "it's a very civilised thing to do on holiday."

"Quite right" said Kate "shall we retire to the patio, do you think?"

"Absolutely" Linda agreed "it's the only place to be when you're drinking cocktails."

Half an hour later the women were almost finished their second drink and there was still no sign of anyone.

"What the hell are those men doing in there?" asked Kate "at this rate it won't be worth going anywhere."

"Couldn't agree more" her sister said brightly "let's just stay here and get legless."

As she finished speaking there was a sudden commotion from the kitchen,

"Watch where you're poking that rod, Phil" Tom was shouting "and mind that box of ……"

There was a clatter as something hit the floor and then silence. Linda rushed to open the kitchen door then closed it again quickly, looking very pale.

She leant against the wall, eyes closed, and whispered,

"Please God – let that be rice."

When they were all finally ready they met outside Mary and Ellen's cottage, only to be delayed yet again.

"I forgot to wash my car window after all" said Ellen "won't be a tick."

She disappeared back into the cottage, and since everyone knew she'd probably be side-tracked again they stood around on the pavement, as it was too hot to sit in the cars.

Linda, Kate and Annie were feeling very mellow by now and had each brought a flask of their chilled cocktails with them which they sipped at happily while they waited.

The older children had been sent to get some sweets for the journey and when they came back ten year old Sarah rushed up to Linda shouting,

"Look mum, I was eating a toffee and my tooth fell out."

Linda squinted at the object in her daughters outstretched hand, trying to focus, then launched into the usual guff about Sarah having to put it under her pillow for the fairies while her daughter looked at her in disbelief.

Before Linda could finish Sarah interrupted scornfully,

"Cut the crap mum, just give me the money."

Phil looked at his daughter in open admiration while the rest of them stepped back a few paces.

Just then Ellen appeared with a bucket of water.

"Sorry I took so long," she said cheerfully "I just thought I'd rinse through some of my smalls while I was at the sink."

So saying, she hurled the contents of the bucket at her car while the others looked on in horror, because Mary was in the passenger seat with the window wide open.

There was a moment of absolute silence, then the car door opened and Mary climbed slowly out.

She stood with her mouth opening and closing like a stranded goldfish, water pouring from her clothes and forming a puddle round her feet.

Eventually she spoke,

"You stupid woman" she spluttered at Ellen "you stupid, stupid woman!"

Then she barged past them all and squelched off up the path.

"I bet I could translate that for you" whispered Phil.

Ellen looked crestfallen.

"I'd better get some towels to dry the seat" she said, turning to follow her sister, then they saw the curtains being pulled shut and heard a key turning in the lock.

"Maybe I'll just borrow some of yours, Linda?" she suggested with a sigh.

After a short debate it was decided to forget the outing for that day at least – much to the mum's delight.

"Right girls," said Linda "party's back at my place."

"But we need some sleep" moaned Phil "who's going to look after the kids?"

"You are buster" answered his wife "it was your idea to go fishing at that ungodly hour, so tough luck."

"What about me?" asked Sam

Kate handed the baby over to him,

"There you go, pal, she's due a feed and she's just filled her nappy."

Before Tom could say anything, Annie pounced,

"And you can forget asking your mum or Aunt Lizzie, 'cos they're invited too."

"How about Mary?" he suggested

"Only if you've got a death wish."

"Well, how about your dad?"

Aunt Lizzie snorted,

"Now you're really clutching at straws."

The rest of the week passed fairly uneventfully and on the last morning they all gathered to say their goodbyes.

"I'm going to miss our little cocktail parties" said Linda "I'll be thinking of you both every morning at 11 o'clock."

"I'll be glad to get back to normal" said Kate, looking decidedly peaky "I haven't got the same stamina as you two."

"There's still a couple of weeks of school holidays" said Annie "we could work on your stamina."

Kate turned even paler.

"Our kids don't go back for a month yet" groaned Linda "I just can't wait to be rid of them again with all their bickering and moaning about being bored."

"Oh, I'll miss having our two around" said Annie "they've come in very handy at times."

"Only because they've been doing your share of the housework for weeks" said Tom, caustically "now you'll have to do it yourself again."

"The hell I will" replied his wife.

"Situation normal there then" said Aunt Lizzie.

CHAPTER FIFTEEN

The following Friday Tom suggested over breakfast that as the school holidays were nearly over, they should have a camping weekend.

Annie looked startled,

"What, in a tent, you mean?"

Lee and his dad rolled their eyes at each other.

"Well no, actually, I thought we'd just do it cowboy style and sleep beneath the stars."

"Don't be so piggin' sarcastic" said Annie "it's just you know I'm not very good at sleeping on the ground – too close to the creepy crawlies and such, they get everywhere."

"You could always wear a wetsuit and a pair of Marigolds" suggested Tom, and got a soggy dishcloth slapped round his head for his trouble.

"How about taking the caravan?" Lee suggested

Aunt Lizzie snorted,

"That old bucket wouldn't get past the end of the lane."

"Not at all" said Tom "there's plenty of life in the old girl yet, and we can use the Cub's minibus to tow it."

Now it was Jade's turn to look dubious,

"Would we have to go through the village?" she asked.

Tom gave up,

"Ok, forget it, I just thought you'd like one last weekend away before going back to school."

After some more debate it was agreed that they would go, but only as far as Sam and Kate's farmland, so they wouldn't be on main roads and should be there by lunch time.

Two hours later they were ready to leave and the old caravan had been hitched to the even older minibus that was stored in one of the disused farm buildings.

"It's only the paint that's holding those two wrecks together" commented Aunt Lizzie "they'll never make the hills."

"Stop being so bloody defeatist and get in" shouted Tom, over the revving of the engine.

Rory was strapped into his seat near the front with his mum and gabbled away excitedly, as they waved goodbye to Grandad, who was animal sitting for them.

The others were belted in at the back, except for Jade, who had insisted on sitting on the floor between the seats with a blanket over her head.

"If you stop for petrol in the village, you're a dead man" she threatened her dad, in a muffled voice.

Their journey was slow and steady, Tom's main problem being trying to keep up sufficient speed to negotiate the hills and having to brake suddenly a couple of times to avoid stray sheep on the road, but they made it in the end.

Since it was now lunchtime Annie volunteered to prepare it while the others got the caravan in place and put up a couple of small tents. All her job entailed was opening half a dozen or so tins of potatoes, meat and vegetables, chucking them all into one big saucepan to heat and buttering a loaf of bread for dipping in the gravy.

Afterwards Jade and Lee were quite happy to wash all the dishes as this was done in the nearby stream which involved much paddling and splashing that Rory could also join in with.

The next stage was where Tom came into his own, organising the campfire.

He had been an assistant Cub leader for a couple of years now, having taken on the job when Lee had first joined, and he took it very seriously. Annie personally thought it was nothing short of masochistic, volunteering to spend several hours a week, not to mention various camping weekends, in the company of two dozen eight to twelve-year old boys.

He was very proud of his official title of Bagheera and was not impressed whenever he overheard them referring to him as 'Baggy' for short.

In no time at all he had them gathering a pile of stones to form a circle for the fire – even Rory had a go by trotting to and fro with a few pebbles, but called a halt on Aunt Lizzie when she staggered up with one that was more the size of a boulder.

When Tom suggested she might be better to start gathering sticks now she went off in a huff.

"I suppose it's time I tried out that dodgy toilet" she muttered to Annie on her way past.

She came back a few minutes later to say she wasn't at all impressed with their chemical loo and that it was about time they fixed the window.

Tom had put his shoulder through the window some time ago on one occasion when they were trying to heave it out of a muddy ditch, and they'd made do with a piece of hardboard in the gap ever since.

An hour or so later Tom was finally satisfied. He had cut out the turfs and put them neatly to one side, then formed a stone circle round the edges of the gap and felt that the large stack of sticks and branches everyone had gathered would be enough to keep the fire going for tonight at least.

"Any minute now he'll be asking us to hoist a flag." moaned Aunt Lizzie.

"If he does, I might just tell him where to stick it." said Annie.

Kate and Sam joined them for a barbeque at tea-time, bringing Adam and Amy and a good supply of wine and beer. Adam was almost three now, so he ran around playing with the others while Amy was content to be surrounded by her soft toys in the portable cot.

It didn't take long for them all to become quite mellow and they sat around discussing recent events, their holiday and even back to Tom's party.

"Have you seen much of Harry since then?" asked Sam.

"He's been popping in quite a bit lately, mainly for some company I think" said Annie "but several times it's been to return Cinders 'cos she keeps hiding in his car."

"I bet Nancy's overjoyed about that" Sam laughed.

"We haven't worked out if Cinders is stalking her or if it's just because she likes Harry so much" said Tom.

When it began to get dark the children gathered round to toast marshmallows on the fire then the younger ones were put to bed in the caravan.

Jade and Lee stayed with the grown-ups until they all began to reminisce about the old days, at which point they happily went off to their tents with a torch each so they could read till they fell asleep.

Some time after midnight Aunt Lizzie went off to use the loo and the others watched her erratic departure with amusement.

They continued to talk for a while until it was noticed that the old lady had been gone for some considerable time, so the two sisters went to see if she'd nodded off somewhere.

As they weaved their way towards the caravan, they heard an urgent voice from the rear,

"Psst, is that you, you daft buggers" the old lady whispered loudly.

Annie and Kate peered in through the louvred slats that were all that remained of the original toilet window.

By the dim glow of the lamp inside Aunt Lizzie peered owlishly back.

"I'm having a bit of trouble with suction here" she said "my bum's stuck."

She was more than a bit miffed at Annie and Kate's reaction because she had to sit there for a further five minutes until they composed themselves enough to suggest that she pull the handle out at the front to release the vacuum.

CHAPTER SIXTEEN

The caravan survived the trip home, much to everyone's relief and it was just as well because Harry moved into it the following weekend.

He came quietly and without any fuss and as soon as he arrived Cinders packed her bags and moved in with him.

From then on she could be seen on guard duty night and day, either perched on the step or peering through the windows, ready to repel all boarders.

Harry quickly became part of the family and insisted on doing his share of the housework, cooking and shopping, so Annie was in seventh heaven.

"He's got the hang of all the clapped-out old gadgets already" she reported to Kate a few days later "he's even offered to repair one or two of them."

"That would be a novelty" her sister retorted "maybe he could start by fixing that bloody cooker of yours."

She was referring to the fact that one of the rings was faulty and if it was turned on by mistake it tripped the mains switch, very often plunging the house into darkness.

"Steady on," said Annie "if he went round fixing *everything* what would we do for entertainment?"

Since autumn was now upon them Annie spent a lot less time in the garden and more hours at her computer. She had been really pleased when her personalised poems had become popular, especially when most of them came from word of mouth recommendations and repeat orders so she had now written dozens, but her main aim was still to finish her novel.

As the book was entirely about her own family, she had no difficulty filling the pages with all their escapades, she often said she could write a chapter a day on all the crazy things that happened to them.

Consequently, she was more often to be found tapping away at her keyboard, eyes glued to the screen and completely oblivious to everything around her.

The others took it in turns to keep the house in order because although they joked with her about her work, they were very supportive really and they all tried to give her the peace and quiet she needed to get on with it.

However, on one particular morning Jade decided it was time to take her mum in hand about her bad habits when she brought Annie a cup of tea and had to cough her way through a cloud of cigarette smoke.

"I've told you before not to come in here" said Annie "just leave the tea outside and shout through the door."

Jade opened the window wide and flapped her hands about.

"Really mum," she said sternly "you smoke and drink far too much, you don't eat properly and now you're not gardening you hardly ever get out for some fresh air."

"I think there's a bit of role reversal here" said Annie "shouldn't I be saying all that to you?"

Jade's screwed up her face in disgust.

"You'll never have to nag me about smoking" she said "it's such a *gross* habit."

"I couldn't agree with you more" said her mum, reaching for her packet of Camel's "now bugger off and leave me alone."

Jade went out of the room muttering and closed the door firmly behind her.

In some ways she was glad her mum chose to completely cut herself off in her study while she was writing because she would be mortified if any of her friends saw her in this state. With the combination of her glazed expression, mouth half open in concentration or talking to herself, and a variety of pens sticking out of her piled up hairstyle or from behind her ears, Jade was pretty sure that her friends would only visit once and never return.

But Jade was not to be put off, so a few days later she went in again with tea and toast and announced that her mum needed a day out for some fresh air and exercise.

"I don't like the sound of that" said Annie,

"So, I've organised a day's trekking for us both" her daughter continued.

Annie's toast went down the wrong way.

"What the hell possessed you to do that" she choked.

Jade looked hurt,

"I just thought it was something a bit different – and you've often said you like horses."

"I do, but I prefer them from a distance" said Annie "their teeth don't look so big."

Jade got up to leave,

"Fine then, if that's how you feel, just forget it."

Annie was immediately contrite, just as her daughter had planned,

"No, it's OK, we'll go – it might be quite a laugh really" she said, trying to sound enthusiastic.

Jade left the room looking smug – she was really getting the hang of this guilt thing.

It was only seven o' clock the following Saturday morning when they got up to be greeted by a cold, wet mist.

"We can't go out in this" Annie declared "we won't be able to see where we're going."

"Don't worry mum" said Jade "it will have cleared by the time we get there."

"What if it snows?"

"Hardly likely, it's only September."

"I think I'm getting a migraine."

"You've never had one in your life."

"My vision's a bit blurred."

"That's just drink and old age" said Jade "now get in the piggin' car and let's go."

When they arrived at the stables there was a lot of frantic activity, so they stood watching for a while as half a dozen horses were saddled up.

One girl, who was obviously in charge, stood in the centre of the yard barking orders in all directions till she was finally satisfied, then she walked over and barked at them.

"My name's Penny, you'll be the ones who want to go hacking I suppose."

Annie could feel Jade's eyes boring into the back of her head, so she bit back the reply she really wanted to give and said,

"That's right, we're beginners."

"You don't say," was Penny's scathing response as she looked them up and down.

"Right, I know which horses will suit you, follow me."

As she turned and walked briskly away Jade whispered,

"What's her problem?"

"I expect it's because we weren't born with riding hats welded to our heads" her mum muttered in reply.

The closer they got, the bigger the animals became, and Annie watched as Penny adjusted the straps on a beast that was obviously a descendant of the Trojan horse. At the same time she tried to avoid making eye contact with the animal in case it should see the blind terror in hers.

"So, what's its name then?" she asked, as if she really cared.

"*His* name is Jake," Penny retorted "short for Jacob's Ladder, he's ready now so I'll give you a leg up."

Annie couldn't help thinking that a ladder should have been part of the deal but said nothing and put her foot into Penny's cupped hands.

The next second she felt herself flying upwards as she was tossed into the saddle and landed heavily, straddling the horse but with her upper body lying parallel to it's back.

It was hardly a dignified position but at least she hadn't shot over the other side as she'd feared might happen, so she sat up quickly and grabbed the reins.

"Not so tightly" Penny snapped "just try and imagine you're holding a jug of water in each hand – and for Pete's sake, relax."

Annie looked down on her from a very great height and refrained from saying she'd rather it was jugs of brandy, because Penny was quite obviously devoid of a sense of humour.

"Right, we'll work you on the lunge rope for a while – you'll have to get the hang of the reins, how to sit properly and how to keep your feet in the stirrups."

"How about how to cope with a nose bleed as well," muttered Annie who was now thinking that an oxygen mask should also have been part of the deal.

All other thoughts fled in the next moment though, as the Sherman tank beneath her began to move forward, so she held on for dear life while they trotted round and round in circles.

"Keep your heels down, toes up, remember the jugs and straighten your backs," Penny called every now and then.

Annie heard and obeyed as best she could with her breakfast churning around in her stomach and her eyes tightly shut.

After about twenty minutes, and just when Annie was convinced she was going to see her bacon and eggs again, Penny grudgingly announced it was time they were off.

A short while later Annie was beginning to think things weren't so bad after all.

After leaving the stables they had ambled along a dirt track for a mile or so, going gradually uphill and through a wood before coming out onto open moorland.

By now the mist had lifted, the sun was shining, and it was a perfect September morning.

Annie had also relaxed sufficiently to be able to hold a conversation, so she and Jade admired the spectacular views and chatted for a while as they moved along side by side.

The only two problems that Annie was experiencing were the flies that constantly buzzed round them and the fact, contrary to what she'd believed, she wasn't going to have to wait till the morning to feel saddle sore.

"I'd swear this thing is made of granite," she moaned, easing herself up in the stirrups to get a moments relief.

Her daughter was showing no such ill effects however, so when Penny trotted back to tell them they were now going to speed up, Jade was happy to oblige.

Annie knew that the instructor was well aware of her discomfort but was damned if she'd give her the satisfaction of saying so.

"Are you ready then?" Penny asked sneeringly.

"I can hardly contain my excitement" said Annie through gritted teeth.

The next moment, after a sharp command from Penny, they were off across the moors at a gallop.

Annie felt the wind whistling round her ears, the sheer agony of her backside crashing up and down in the saddle and the sensation of some fillings coming loose.

Many thoughts flashed through her mind at that point, most of them containing expletives, but she hung on grimly for two reasons.

Firstly, because she was determined to survive long enough to get her hands round Penny's throat and secondly because she didn't know where the brake was.

When they finally pulled up it was only the pleading expression on Jade's face that stopped her from launching herself across at Penny and bearing her to the ground.

The journey back was slow and painful but Annie said not a word, although she was greatly relieved to see Tom waiting for them as they entered the yard.

Penny leapt nimbly to the ground and called for the others to dismount as she led her horse away without so much as a backward glance.

However, when Annie tried to follow suit and manage to slide clumsily to the ground, she discovered she'd lost the use of her legs and held on desperately to Jake's stirrup to stop herself falling flat on her face.

Tom and Jade reached her just as a stable hand came to lead the horse away, so she then had to clutch at Tom's arm for support while she tried to put one foot in front of the other.

"Thought I'd just take a hike over here to drive you both home" he said cheerfully "how did it go?"

Before Annie had a chance to reply a cat suddenly ran screeching across the yard, followed by a barking dog, and several of the horses reared in panic.

Annie then had the immense satisfaction of seeing Penny dive to avoid flailing hooves and land face down in a pile of steaming manure.

Mother and daughter looked at each other,

"Wish I'd caught that on my phone" said Jade "could have put it on YouTube."

It took three days and several hot baths before Annie stopped walking like John Wayne and she eventually stopped twitching at the mention of all things equine, so when Jade finally confessed that she's got herself a weekend job at the stables her mum's only response was that at least the horseshit would be good for the garden.

CHAPTER SEVENTEEN

By mid-October the weather had taken a definite turn for the worse and everyone's mood was affected.

Jade and Lee were on half term holiday and were constantly bickering because they were bored from being stuck indoors.

Annie's temper was also beginning to fray and she was fed up with their arguments constantly interrupting her when she was writing.

"Mum, will you tell Lee to stop barging into my room" Jade complained one morning "he doesn't even knock."

"Well put a bolt on it then – there's bound to be one in your dad's workshop."

"Can't dad do it for me?"

"No, he bloody well can't, he's in bed with a migraine."

"Do I need to use a screwdriver?"

"I think you'll find it helps."

"What size?"

"I don't know, you'll have to find the right screws first then use one that fits them."

"Sounds a bit complicated to me."

Lee charged in just then and Jade immediately flounced out, pushing him roughly aside as she left.

"Mum, did you see that?" Lee whined "she nearly broke my arm."

"Well, you've got another one."

"Oh, that's great – *she* doesn't even get told off."

"Did you want something Lee?" his mum asked, through gritted teeth.

"I only came to tell you that Grandad's here and he's in a rotten mood."

Annie sighed and got up from her desk,

"This day is just getting better by the minute"

In the kitchen Aunt Lizzie and her dad had already fallen out and were ignoring each other.

"The miserable old bugger is having a go at me because we haven't cut the grass for a while" fumed the old lady.

"The lawnmower's broken again and it's too wet anyway" said Annie shortly.

"It's too bloody long as well" Grandad snapped "you'd need a scythe to cut it now."

"There's one in the back of the coal shed."

"It'll be blunt, no doubt."

"So sharpen it then."

"I'll just bloody well do that – there's damn all else to do round here."

After he'd stormed out the two women sat drinking coffee and moaning about the weather, stroppy kids and grumpy old men.

Eventually Grandad returned, wielding the freshly sharpened scythe like a Samurai warrior.

"Watch what you're doing, you daft old sod" cried Aunt Lizzie, moving nimbly to the far side of the room.

"It's a bit nippy out there" said Grandad.

"There's an old dufflecoat of Tom's in the hall" said Annie "it'll be a bit big but it's better than nothing."

Her dad disappeared again.

"Do you reckon it's wise to let him loose with that thing?" asked Aunt Lizzie.

"He'll be fine" said Annie "the worst he could do is cut his leg off"

Half an hour later Tom staggered through, bleary eyed.

"How's the head?" asked his wife

"On a scale of one to ten it's about twelve" said Tom, fumbling for the switch on the kettle.

At the same time he glanced out of the window and saw Annie's dad standing in the middle of the lawn, leaning on the scythe and with the hood of his coat hiding most of his face,

"Bloody hell" he whispered hoarsely "it was only a migraine – I wasn't expecting the Grim Reaper."

A few days later Aunt Lizzie was standing in the kitchen staring out of the window.

"Bloody silly time of year to be doing that" she said.

She was watching as Tom, Harry and Lee struggled to pitch a tent on the lawn and although for once it wasn't raining there was a strong, gusting wind that was making their task more difficult.

"Well, you know Tom," said Annie "he's like a kid with a new toy."

Tom had recently done a deal with a local camping shop and bought half a dozen new tents for the Cubs. That morning he'd decided they should try and put one up to see if they really were as easy to erect as the shop claimed.

"They won't even be camping till next summer" said Aunt Lizzie "why the hell couldn't he wait till nearer the time?"

"Oh, they're thinking of having one next weekend apparently, poor wee buggers, although some of them are proper little sods, so maybe it will serve them right."

The task was eventually completed and the three of them trooped into the kitchen in search of hot food and drinks, Lee limping badly.

In answer to Annie's questioning look Harry explained,

"He missed the peg with the mallet."

"What a wally" said Aunt Lizzie.

They collapsed round the table and got stuck into their bowls of soup while they discussed the merits of the new tents and agreed they were much quicker to put up than the old canvas ones the Cubs had had for at least a decade.

"They'll be much easier to carry as well," said Tom "they're so lightweight."

"You can say that again" said Aunt Lizzie

"How would you know?" asked Lee

"Because the bloody thing has just flown past the window" the old lady sniggered.

They all ran out of the back door in time to see the tent sail over the garden wall and head across the yard in the direction of the river.

"Come on" shouted Tom "we have to catch it before it goes over the other wall."

The men chased after it at high speed while the women watched, Jade had also appeared, carrying Rory, wondering what all the noise was about.

Just as they'd almost reached the tent another gust of wind carried it further away.

"If they're not careful I can see the three of them paragliding over the village in a minute" Aunt Lizzie commented.

"Well, let's hope they have the sense to pull their hats down over their faces so that no-one recognises them" said Annie.

Jade turned to her baby brother and shook her head sadly,

"If only we were old enough to emigrate" she moaned.

CHAPTER EIGHTEEN

It was November 5th and, because they never passed up an excuse to have a party, Annie had issued a dozen or so invitations and promised that theirs would be the biggest bonfire for miles. Sophie and Cinders were to have a sleepover with Carol.

In the afternoon she watched with great satisfaction as the men piled piece after piece of old furniture on to the rapidly growing pile.

Aunt Lizzie was horrified.

"What are you putting that kitchen unit on there for?" she asked

"The doors kept jumping off their runners and the drawers were falling to bits" said Annie.

"What about that mattress?"

"It was Sophie's – she ate most of it."

"That sideboard looks OK to me."

"Woodworm" countered Annie.

"You'll have nothing left in the house at this rate."

"Who cares – it's mostly all crap anyway."

Aunt Lizzie gave up and went indoors just as Grandad arrived on his bike.

"What the hell are you doing with that sideboard?" he demanded

Annie turned to Jade

"You've heard the script – you tell him" she said, then followed her aunt into the kitchen.

"Right, time to get the tables and chairs set up then I'll get started on the booze."

"You'll be making that awful stuff with the twigs in it then?" said Aunt Lizzie.

"I'll have you know my mulled wine and spiced cider are famous round here" Annie retorted, "people come for miles just to taste it."

"Oh, I know that" replied the old lady "it's just that they have a hell of a job getting home afterwards."

There were over twenty people gathered by the time it was dark enough to light the fire but despite the fact there was so much rotten old wood on it Tom and Harry were having difficulty getting it going and were being treated to Grandad's usual advice wherever fires were concerned.

"Just chuck some bloody petrol on it" he yelled across at them "that'll get it going."

"Maybe so dad" said Kate "but I think they were hoping to contain it within the farmyard."

Half an hour later it was finally blazing and everyone gathered round to warm themselves while Tom and Harry took a break for a drink before lighting the fireworks.

"What a lot of palaver over nothing" Grandad was moaning "and you haven't even got a proper guy, it's just a couple of old black sacks stuffed with straw – I could have done a better job than that."

The two other men looked at each other.

"We'll be thinking the same thing I expect" said Harry.

"Tempting" said Tom "very tempting."

Shortly afterwards the fireworks were ignited, the men taking it in turns to light them and everyone but Grandad admired the display.

"Bloody waste of money if you want my opinion."

"We don't" said Annie and Kate in unison.

"All they do is fart, fizzle and go out" he continued.

"Shut up and have a sparkler" said Aunt Lizzie, shoving a lit one into his hand.

"What the hell am I supposed to do with this?" he snapped.

His daughters exchanged glances,

"Will you tell him or shall I?" muttered Kate.

Some time later Tom called out that they were lighting the last firework.

"I've saved the biggest and best till last" he shouted, as he lit the touchpaper on the rocket and moved away.

It went off with a shower of sparks, an ear-splitting bang and a very impressive display of shapes and colours that earned a round of applause from all but one of the audience.

"What a load of bloody fuss over nothing" Grandad proclaimed loudly.

"If we'd thought about it sooner we could have attached that rocket to the back of his coat" Aunt Lizzie whispered.

As the men approached Grandad repeated his observations.

"I was just saying that was a lot of fuss over nothing – I could have made better ones myself."

"Oh, I don't doubt that for a minute" said Tom "but I think there's a law against making Molotov cocktails."

"So there should be" said Aunt Lizzie "they're dangerous things them."

"Of course they're dangerous, you daft old bat – they're designed to maim and kill."

"Oh, that's stretching it a bit" said the old lady with a twinkle in her eye "but I did get one of those little umbrellas stuck up my nose once"

After the bonfire it rained non-stop for days and Annie was feeling thoroughly cheesed off one morning while she sat with Rory, having breakfast. He'd had a cold for two days now and was very snuffly and sneezy, but still as cheerful as always.

"Wouldn't it be nice to be packing our cases and heading off to a hot country right now?" his mum asked him.

"Naaa" Rory said, grinning.

"We could go surfing on Bondi beach" she suggested.

"Mmm" said Rory, and shovelled another spoonful of cereal into his mouth.

"OK, how about you and me taking off on safari to see a few elephants?"

There was a small explosion from the high-chair and Annie's face was suddenly covered in a gloopy mess. She reached for the pack of wet wipes and smiled,

"There's nothing quite like a Weetabix sneeze to start the day right, is there honey?"

As she was cleaning them both up Lee came hopping barefoot into the kitchen and made his way straight through to the bathroom.

When he returned Annie eyed him quizzically.

"There's a couple of frogs in the hall" he said, by way of explanation "but one of them is a bit flat now."

Annie sighed.

At this time of year they often saw dozens of frogs out in the farmyard and, because there was a gap at the bottom of their front door, they would occasionally find a one or two small ones in the hall.

She went to the cupboard under the sink and pulled out a plastic container just as Jade charged in, looking thunderous.

Annie could tell that her daughter had woken up having a 'teen moment' which was how the family described her moods. Unfortunately, these moments seemed to all run together sometimes and she could be stroppy for days if she so decided.

Jade slammed a bowl on the table then bent down to get cereal out of the cupboard while her mum watched, saying nothing.

Her brother had no such sense of course.

"I just squished a frog with my bare foot" he grinned.

His sister turned on him with a look that would have had an all-in wrestler backing into a corner and snarled,

"God, I wish you could be abducted by aliens."

Annie sighed again and went off in search of bodies. She found the flat one easily enough but while she was peering into dark corners for the other one, she heard a blood-curdling scream from the kitchen.

As she rushed back through she heard doors opening upstairs and the sound of running footsteps and by the time she got there Tom was right behind her with Aunt Lizzie a very close second.

Jade was scrunched into a tiny space between the fridge and the sink with her hands over her mouth and her eyes popping.

Lee had his head down on the table and was banging his fists on it while his shoulders shook.

"Well?" Annie demanded finally.

Her son looked up at them with tears streaming down his face and eventually managed to gasp,

"It's no big deal, mum – she just found a frog in her Fruit 'n' Fibre."

CHAPTER NINETEEN

It was 6am on a Saturday morning early in December and there were twelve of them gathered in the kitchen, most of them half asleep and the rest of them grumpy.

"Remind me again whose bloody silly idea this was" moaned Tom.

"YOURS!" shouted several voices in unison.

A few days ago Tom had come up with the suggestion that they should all get together for a trip to the city to do Christmas shopping.

The idea had been readily accepted at the time but now that the day was upon them it was a very different story.

Outside it was still pitch dark with a bitter cold wind and icy rain so most of them were huddled round the fireplace, even though it was only the dying embers of the previous night's fire.

Jade and Lee were not morning people at the best of times and were both in zombie mode while the youngest three were confused and cranky at being dragged out of their cosy beds in the middle of the night.

"I'm beginning to wish we'd arranged a babysitter for the day" said Kate as she struggled to put a hat and gloves on her daughter for the umpteenth time since leaving their house.

"I know" said Annie "but part of the plan is for them to see Santa, isn't it?"

Grandad snorted,

"Huh, they could see him anytime – there must be a dozen or more of the big jolly buggers in the town shops."

"Actually, I heard there was a shortage of them this year" Lee piped up, smirking "maybe you could apply for the job, Grandad."

The old man glared at him suspiciously while the others kept their eyes averted.

"If he got the job there would be hundreds of children in therapy for the rest of their lives" muttered Harry as they all trooped outside.

They were taking four cars between them in order to have room for all the shopping and Harry had drawn the short straw, so he was being accompanied by Grandad on the two hour journey.

"Good luck son" whispered Aunt Lizzie "but in case it gets too much for you I've slipped a monkey wrench into your glove compartment."

The journey took almost three hours in the end, due to toilet and sickness stops as well as traffic, but eventually the cars all pulled into the huge underground carpark beneath the main shopping centre.

They were able to park on the same level but not next to each other as it was already almost full to capacity and it was agreed that most of the shopping would go in Harry's car at the end of the day.

"I don't know about anyone else but I'm going to start with breakfast" said Tom, "I'm starving."

"Great idea, dad" said Lee "I reckon Jade could just do with a big plate of runny eggs on toast right now."

Jade's face changed to a different shade of green but for once her brother got away with his remark without comment.

They headed for the nearest café and over breakfast discussed splitting into two groups throughout the day and covering only certain shops at a time to avoid the risk of bumping in to each other.

"OK, we women will take the little ones this morning" said Annie "then we'll swop with you men at lunch time"

Her sister kept her eyes lowered and tried not to smirk, knowing the toddlers would be well and truly grumpy by then and in need of their afternoon naps.

"Can I come with you please?" Harry asked the women in a pleading voice.

"Are you insane?" asked Grandad, incredulously "why the hell would you want to trail around the shops with three crazy women and a load of whingeing kids?"

"Because compared to being stuck in a car with you for three hours, we'll be like a breath of fresh air for him" said Aunt Lizzie

By late morning Kate and Annie were feeling very pleased with themselves, having managed to get well over half of the things on their lists and Harry and Aunt Lizzie had done almost as well so they were all in good spirits.

Jade and Lee had been allowed to go off on their own on the strict understanding that even if they fell out they had to stay together and check in by text every so often.

Surprisingly they had been getting on quite well and hadn't argued once so far.

Added to this the women realised they'd got a real bargain with Harry because every time they became laden with bags he would nip back to his car with them.

"That wife of his is a fool" said Aunt Lizzie on one occasion as they watched him disappear into the distance for the third time "he's just one of the nicest men we know."

Annie decided to admit to a little secret.

"They've been seeing each other quite a lot in the past few weeks actually."

The three women looked at each other, shrugged and smiled.

"Here's hoping she's seen sense by now" said Aunt Lizzie.

By the time the women got to the Italian restaurant they'd agreed on for lunch they were feeling very smug as they had more or less finished their shopping and were looking forward to their meal and a glass of wine.

Tom and Sam, however, arrived looking harassed.

"We've lost Grandad" Sam said immediately.

"Was that on purpose?" asked his wife.

"No, honestly," said Tom "one minute he was there with us in a bookshop and the next he was gone."

After a few minutes discussion it was agreed they should give the old man another half hour before sending out search parties.

"He knows this restaurant, we've been here a few times with him" said Kate "let's just look at the menu and order some coffees for now."

There was still no sign of him when they'd finished their drinks and they were all beginning to feel really hungry.

"Let's order anyway" suggested Tom "it will probably take another half hour till they serve it so we can go and look for him then."

He signalled to the waiter who had been hovering expectantly in the background and they began listing their choices.

When it got to Jade's turn she looked coyly up at the good looking young man.

"How much is it for just a plate of chips?" she enquired.

"It depends" was the waiters reply.

Jade smiled.

"It depends on what?" she asked.

The young man looked at her with a confused expression on his face.

"It depends" he repeated.

Jade was slightly flustered now so she looked to her dad for help, whereupon he made the classic mistake of speaking louder and more slowly,

"How – much – is – it – for – a – plate – of – chips ?"

The waiter now turned his attention to Tom and said, even more loudly,

"IT DEPENDS."

Everyone was looking at each other, baffled, other customers were beginning to stare and Tom was about to try one more time when they became aware of Grandad, lurking in the background, watching them all in amazement.

"What's all the bloody fuss about?" he demanded.

"I only asked how much it was for a plate of chips" Jade mumbled in embarrassment.

The old man shook his head in disbelief,

"He's told you three times already, you silly sods – they're eighty pence!"

The women had agreed they would stay for Santa's grotto before taking their child-free break but when they reached the top floor of the department store they were all stunned at the length of the queue.

"There must be at least twenty families in front of us" Tom exclaimed "we'll be lucky if we get to the front in the next hour."

"OK" said Kate "let's forget it and do the town next week."

Unfortunately for them Adam had already seen the grotto up ahead and created a bit of a storm when they tried to leave.

"Right then," Annie announced "we've done our bit so we're going for a coffee now, we'll be back in half an hour."

The men just hunched their shoulders and prepared for the long wait.

By the time the women returned the little ones were seriously cranky, but they were almost at the front of the queue so to save time they all went in together. However, from the moment Amy laid eyes on Santa everything went pear shaped.

She took one look at his big bearded face and let out such a scream of terror that it startled everyone, including most of the shoppers on the top floor, then all at once there was complete bedlam.

Adam immediately rushed to his baby sister's defence and kicked the old man in the shin while Rory, with perfect aim from his buggy, lobbed a full bottle of juice at Santa and caught him right between the eyes.

Sam went to grab his son, but not before Adam had managed to get hold of a handful of beard and tugged with all his might. This was the final straw for Santa as the beard was a real one so, after giving a yelp of pain, he swore loudly.

The four adults grabbed children and buggies and as they exited the grotto, even above the din of Amy's screams, a child's voice could clearly be heard saying,

"I reckon Santa's going to be in big trouble with his mum tonight."

At the arranged time everyone headed back to the car park to load up Harry's boot, which was when Annie realised that Grandad was missing again.

"He was getting fed up and just went off for a walk" said Sam "he said he'd meet us here."

Jade and Lee were left to strap the little ones in while the others packed all the bags away but there was still no sign of Grandad when they were finished.

"You women stay here with the kids" said Tom "we'll split up and take a level each, he's probably in here somewhere."

Twenty minutes later they all came back with the old man in tow.

"He was two floors up" Harry muttered "same make and colour of car, just an older version."

"Forty bloody minutes I waited" Grandad complained "I'm piggin' freezing now."

He climbed stiffly into the car and slammed the door as Harry continued,

"You'd have thought the snarling, slobbering Doberman in the back might have given him a clue, but apparently not."

CHAPTER TWENTY

A few days later Harry told Annie and Tom that he was moving back home and gave them a letter from Nancy.

"I'm just going to start packing my stuff so I'll leave you to read it in your own time" he said "let me know what you think."

It was, first and foremost, an abject apology for her past behaviour and then Nancy asked if they would consider meeting her, so that she could do the same in person.

"What do you think then? asked Tom.

"I reckon it took a bit of courage for her to write this" his wife replied, "and for Harry's sake we should at least give it a try."

Harry's relief was quite touching.

"You wouldn't believe the change in her" he said eagerly "she's almost back to being the woman I married ten years ago – but she's very nervous about meeting you again."

"Let's give it a go" said Annie "but it won't be bone china and cucumber sandwiches, it'll be just us, being ourselves."

"She'd be happy with a mug of builders tea and a bacon buttie right now" Harry beamed "how does tomorrow suit you?"

The meeting was a bit awkward for about five minutes as they greeted each other, Nancy looking very uncomfortable while Harry chattered on a little too brightly – then Rory toddled in from the living room, smiling broadly and gave Nancy a resounding slap on the backside.

"Me done a poo" he announced.

Annie and Tom grinned at each other,

"That's his first proper sentence" Tom said proudly "what a guy."

After looking startled for a moment Nancy's face broke into a bemused smile when her husband started laughing uncontrollably.

"Welcome to the Crazy Gang" he gasped eventually.

After having his nappy changed Rory appeared to have taken an instant shine to Nancy and insisted on sitting on her lap, which she was perfectly happy with, not even seeming to mind when he blew a few yogurt raspberries and kept offering her bits of soggy Marmite toast.

Tom and Harry felt that their presence was no longer needed so they excused themselves after half an hour saying they had to check an oil leak in Harry's car.

Aunt Lizzie had managed to lighten the atmosphere even more by relating a funny incident that had happened in the village shop that morning, so after a while Nancy plucked up the courage to make her apology.

"I can't believe how unspeakably rude I've been in the past" she began hesitantly "you've been such good friends to Harry, he never stops talking about what an amazing, mad family you are. It's no wonder he's preferred to be here these past few months, compared to being in my company, I'm just so happy that he's stuck with it and given me a second chance."

"He's a grand lad" said Aunt Lizzie "and he's part of the family now so we're glad to see him happy as well, he knew a side of you that we've never seen and he persevered, bless him, let's just hope you can cope with us as well as he can."

Nancy smiled,

"I'd be delighted to try" she began, and then stiffened visibly as Cinders strolled into the room.

The cat looked round at them all scornfully, eyes resting on Nancy for a moment, then she stuck her nose in the air and sauntered on through the open back door.

"Good grief" said the old lady "I think you just got over the first hurdle there, dear."

CHAPTER TWENTY ONE

A week before Christmas the families did a mammoth food shop and even Grandad joined them for the day, although no-one was quite sure why because he was his usual grumpy self as they all trundled round the aisles.

Not surprisingly the shop was mobbed.

"All this bloody money being spent just so that people can stuff themselves silly for a few days" he grumbled to Annie.

"It's all part of the festive season, dad" she replied "just eating and drinking and having fun with the family."

"There's nothing funny about having indigestion for a week" he continued to moan.

'We keep telling you to get some new dentures" retorted Annie "then you'll be able to chew your food properly."

She was referring to the fact that her dad had been without his false teeth for several years now, ever since he'd sneezed them over the side of the cross-channel ferry on a day trip to Ireland.

"I'm too old to be breaking in new teeth" he huffed "I've managed without them so far."

"Well, you don't have to join us if you don't want to" replied his daughter "we can always bring your Christmas dinner to you."

Her dad bristled.

"Someone has to be there to keep an eye on the kids while you drink yourselves senseless" he snapped.

They were in the confectionery aisle at this point so Annie took a deep breath, grabbed a bag of humbugs off the shelf and chucked them in his trolley saying,

"There you are dad, treat yourself."

Her dad wandered off eventually and she met up with Tom in the booze section where he was contemplating the wine selection and patiently reading the labels, because he liked to think of himself as a bit of a connoisseur.

"Right, this one's all yours now," Annie announced, as she hauled a dangerously overloaded trolley up behind him "how long have you been here?"

"About half an hour" he replied.

"For pity's sake Tom, if it's twelve per cent or more and less than six quid a bottle just bung it in the trolley."

Tom looked at her sadly and shook his head,

"You're such a Philistine" he sniffed "I don't suppose you'll want to help me choose some bubbly to go with the canapes?"

Annie raised her eyebrows and sighed,

"The only advice you'll get from me is that if you can't pronounce it, we can't afford it" she said, before going off in search of an empty trolley.

Kate was looking harassed when her sister caught up with her in the frozen food section.

"What's up?" asked Annie.

"First they'd sold out of chestnuts, they're completely out of brandy butter and now there's no bloody toffee ice cream" Kate fumed.

"No big deal" said Annie "there's still a week to go."

Her sister growled at her,

"I'm not planning to shop for another month after today – I'd rather give birth than go through this again – and if I hear 'Jingle Bells' one more time I'm going to go for someone's jugular."

Annie looked at her sister in surprise.

"If you catch up with dad he's got a nice bag of sweets you can share" she said, before moving swiftly on.

She found Jade pushing Rory in a trolley through the baking aisle, ticking off her own list and in surprisingly good humour.

"We're nearly finished and we've had a great time, haven't we Rory?" she beamed at her baby brother as she wiped a foamy beard from his chin where he'd sucked the corner off a box of icing sugar, "he looks like a mini Santa, don't you think?"

Rory blew a frothy raspberry and grabbed a bottle of vodka from a passing trolley.

His mum grabbed it back and smiled apologetically at the other shopper,

"Sorry about that, he's really a whisky drinker to be honest."

The man just looked alarmed and accelerated up the aisle.

"Some people have no sense of humour" said Jade "anyway, where is everybody?"

"Grandad's gone for a cuppa, your dad's choosing the booze, Kate is busy defrosting the freezer section and Sam is still hiding in the creche with their two."

Jade nodded and then looked at her mum with a hint of a smirk before saying,

"Last I saw of Aunt Lizzie she was mopping up Lee's blood."

"WHAT?"

"Don't panic mum, he's OK, I think he was more embarrassed at the fuss Aunt Lizzie was making cos he only fell and whacked his nose on the trolley."

"How the hell did he manage to do that?"

Jade's mouth twitched ever so slightly as she looked her mum straight in the eye and said,

"He slipped on a grape, apparently."

They all met for lunch in the cafeteria and agreed they'd had enough for the day.

"I've got everything on my list anyway" said Annie.

"Stop being so bloody smug" her sister said wearily "I bet there will be something you've forgotten and you'll have to come in again before next week."

Annie ignored Kate's remark and snapped a cucumber in half for Rory.

"That child will be burping all afternoon" Aunt Lizzie said caustically "poor wee soul."

"It keeps him quiet" said Annie "and it's healthier than sweets or crisps."

"I know, but it's not normal is it, people keep giving us funny looks."

"After all the years you've lived with us, you should be well used to that."

The old lady surveyed the table and took in the sight of Sam wiping yoghurt off his face with a terry nappy after feeding Amy, Grandad dunking a lump of baguette in his tea to soften it and Lee trying to eat a burger with a huge wad of tissue stuck up his nose and then she smiled

"You're right, of course, and I wouldn't have it any other way."

Half an hour later they all trundled across the car park with five loaded trolleys and started filling the car boots.

As the last bag was finally in place they all heaved a sigh of relief, then Annie turned to Tom and whispered urgently,

"I've just got to nip back inside for a minute."

"Oh, for Pete's sake woman, you're a big girl now, can't you wait till we get home?"

His wife backed away swiftly, checking to see if any of the others were listening,

"I don't need the loo, you wally" she grinned sheepishly "I forgot to buy the bloody turkey."

That night, after the children were all asleep, Annie and Tom spent a couple of hours putting up the tree and decorations. Their tradition was to also consume a bottle of spiced rum between them, much to Aunt Lizzie's disapproval, and she anxiously plied them with plates of nibbles throughout the evening to soak up the alcohol.

When they'd finished Tom and Annie insisted that she join them, lying flat on the floor in the middle of the room to see how evenly spaced the ceiling decorations were and she had to reluctantly agree that they were completely symmetrical.

"We've perfected it over the years" Annie slurred "got it down to a fine art now."

Tom lurched to his feet and made his way to the kitchen to refill their glasses, burping loudly as he went.

At the same time Annie hiccupped, Cinders sneezed and Sophie farted spectacularly,

"Sounds like you've been training your own symphony orchestra as well" said the old lady.

CHAPTER TWENTY TWO

Over the next few days things were pretty hectic as everyone worked their way through Annie's chore list, which was three pages long, as well as the need to wait till the children were in bed to wrap and hide presents, which sometimes meant being up till the wee small hours if they didn't go to sleep when expected.

On Christmas Eve Annie and Aunt Lizzie, starting at 7am, spent the morning baking sausage rolls, mince pies and mini pizzas while Jade baked chocolate brownies and a gingerbread house. Annie had also made her famous stuffing which was actually in the form of a meatloaf that she baked in advance and kept foil wrapped in the fridge.

Nancy had dropped in a couple of times for coffee over the past two weeks, she was now getting quite used to the eccentricities of the family and seemed to genuinely enjoy the time she spent with them. She and Harry had been invited for Christmas dinner and insisted they wanted to help with some of the preparations, so they'd agreed to come for lunch and spend the afternoon working through whatever was left on the list.

Nancy was almost speechless when she saw the trays full of baking that were on every surface in the kitchen.

"It smells fantastic in here" she exclaimed "there's enough food to start your own bakery."

"Hah" retorted Aunt Lizzie "if we left the menfolk and the kids alone in here it would be gone within the hour, they'd go through it like a plague of locusts."

"I was going to offer to bake something as well" said Nancy "but it looks like you've got everything covered."

"Not everything" said Annie "how are you at making shortbread?"

"She's a really good cook" Harry chipped in "and her baking is amazing too."

Nancy shook her head at her husband, looking embarrassed,

"It's just something I've always enjoyed, not exactly Masterclass standard though, Harry's exaggerating a bit, but I've already made shortbread so I'll bring a box tomorrow"

"That would be grand" said Aunt Lizzie "and now I think most of this stuff is cool enough to store – who's going to be brave enough to open the cupboard?"

Nancy looked at her questioningly.

"Not me, that's for sure" said Jade, heading for the utility room with a tray full of gingerbread shapes "I've got to finish my house and there's no room in here."

Lee had just wandered into the kitchen with Rory, his nose having followed the smell of baking,

"I'll open it" he said cheerfully, and reached for the handle of the tall narrow cupboard by the fridge"

"Do it slowly" cried his mum and Aunt Lizzie in unison, but too late, Lee had already wrenched the door open and stepped quickly aside as a cascade of Tupperware containers rained onto the floor, lids popping off and flying everywhere.

Annie sighed deeply,

"I spent piggin' ages fitting all the right lids yesterday – I hate doing it, it's like something out of the Krypton factor."

Nancy was highly amused,

"Not to worry," she laughed "that sort of job is right up my street – just shows you how sad I am!"

In no time at all a dozen boxes were filled, leaving a generous amount out on plates for lunch and half an hour later, when everyone was seated round the table, Jade produced her finished gingerbread house which earned a round of applause.

The house was beautifully decorated with chocolate button roof tiles, icicles hanging from the eaves and stained glass windows, there was a small LED tea light inside which glowed cosily through the coloured panes and the snow covered garden had a Christmas tree bedecked with baubles and tiny fairy lights and a snowman complete with mouth, nose and eyes and finished off with a hat and scarf.

"That's fabulous Jade" said Nancy 'it's beautifully detailed and looks so professional, people would pay a lot of money for something like that."

Jade looked pleased but embarrassed, especially when Tom went on to boast,

"She's always been very artistic, you should see some of the things she's hand-made for presents over the years, a lot of it personalised as well, which is a real selling point – if she ever decided to start up in business."

Annie could see that Jade was squirming by now so she announced it was time to eat, giving her daughter the chance to sidle out of the room to put the house on display in the sitting room, up on a high shelf, well out of reach of Rory and Sophie and, hopefully, Cinders.

While they were all tucking into pizza, sausage rolls, cheese and home-made chutney, Annie produced the chore list which was now only one A4 page long but still caused a good-natured groan from the family.

"It's not as bad as it looks" said Annie "some of them will only take five minutes and we've got two extra pairs of hands this year."

Over the next few hours they all got stuck in to their various chores, Nancy and Aunt Lizzie choosing to sit at the table preparing all the vegetables, which was no mean feat as there would be fourteen for dinner the following day.

While the old lady worked her way through a sack of potatoes Nancy peeled parsnips, carrots and sprouts then moved on to the cauliflower and broccoli, Aunt Lizzie remarking that it was like being on punishment in the army.

"It does look as if we're feeding an army" Nancy laughed "even with fourteen of us we'll never get through this lot in one go."

"Ah, but that's the plan" Annie chipped in on her way to the utility room with a big pile of bedding "it will keep us in bubble and squeak and magic soup for days after as well."

Before Nancy had to ask, Aunt Lizzie explained,

"That's when she chucks all the veg in a blender with some stock, the kids don't see exactly what goes in but they love it, and they don't even realise they're eating sprouts as well."

"Very sneaky but also healthy – makes good sense" agreed Nancy.

Tom and Harry had been on outdoor duty splitting logs and kindling to last a week at least and filling extra coal buckets, all of which were stacked on pallets by the back door and covered with a tarpaulin.

"Never know what the weather will do" Tom had said "it could be lashing down for a week and it saves the trek across to the coal shed."

Jade and Lee had been given strict instructions to get their rooms properly tidied while keeping Rory amused at the same time.

"And I'll be doing a thorough check when you've finished" warned their mum "so don't go cramming stuff into cupboards and under beds 'cos they'll be the first places I'll be looking."

By four o'clock Annie was happy to announce that she was on the very last chore and that was the kedgeree she was about to make for tea.

"Then it's early to bed for the kids while we watch 'It's a Wonderful Life', with lots of chocolate, alcohol and a box of tissues – and you're very welcome to join us if you wish" she said to Harry and Nancy.

When Nancy looked as if she was about to accept the invitation Harry hastily declined,

"Kind of you to offer" he said "but it would be safer for us to leave now – otherwise we might not make it for dinner tomorrow!"

CHAPTER TWENTY THREE

On Christmas morning they were all startled awake at 6am by the sound of Lee running through the house, ringing a large ornamental brass bell and yelling 'Ho Ho Ho' at the top of his voice.

As the children all piled into bed with their mum and dad, Tom muttered quietly to Annie,

"If it wasn't Christmas Day, I'd have caught him by the clapper and he'd be hanging over the banister by his ankles right now"

"If it wasn't Christmas Day he wouldn't have done it, you pillock" his wife whispered back, then turned her attention to the ritual of opening their stockings, Aunt Lizzie having joined them, perched precariously on the end of the bed and looking slightly stunned.

"I've put the kettle on" she mumbled "at least I think I did, 'cos I definitely went into the kitchen - but it might have been a dream."

"No problem" said Annie "this will only take about ten minutes the way our lot attack their pressies."

Sure enough, just fifteen minutes later Aunt Lizzie was stuffing a bin liner with wrapping paper which she carried through to the kitchen while the others were still chomping on chocolate coins and slurping fizzy drinks.

By the time the tea was ready they were all in the sitting room, Jade and Lee sorting the bigger presents into piles, Annie grappling with Rory who was just desperate to tear more paper and meanwhile Tom headed for the kitchen to turn the oven on.

For over an hour all was chaos while the main presents were revealed, one of which was a toy tractor and trailer for Rory that caused much amusement while he got the hang of it, a space having to be cleared across the living room floor and the door opened into the hallway.

"Just think Annie," said Tom "you could train him to be your delivery boy and he could bring your meals to the study, then you could stay welded to your seat for the whole day."

"Now why would she force Rory into child labour when she's already got four other people to do that for her" Aunt Lizzie said drily.

When the second load of wrapping paper had been disposed of and bacon rolls consumed with more tea, Tom announced he was heading for the kitchen and that he was not to be disturbed unless he called for help.

"Suits me fine" said his wife, turning to Aunt Lizzie "fancy a sherry?"

An hour later all was calm, the fire had been lit, Jade and Lee were in zombie mode playing their new computer games and Rory was fast asleep in the huge box his tractor had come in. The women had settled on the sofa with their glasses of sherry, watching 'Love Actually' on the telly and Tom was happy in the kitchen with his CD on at full volume while he worked away at his own chore list for dinner and kept an eye on the turkey.

At ten o' clock Tom discovered the two women sound asleep and snoring, his eldest children still oblivious to the world around them and that Rory had woken up and munched his way through half a selection box. He now had Cinders in a headlock, trying to force a Curly Wurly through her tightly clenched teeth and Sophie was behind the sofa, chewing her way through the draught excluder that had once been a stuffed caterpillar.

Tom sighed deeply then went over to the music centre, turned the volume up high and for the second time that morning the women were rudely awoken, this time by Guns 'n' Roses singing 'Sweet Child of Mine'.

"Right," yelled Tom, "time to get a move on, folk will be arriving in a couple of hours."

Jade and Lee were ordered to switch their games off and come and help with bread sauce and pigs in blankets, Aunt Lizzie started clearing away the sherry and glasses and Annie staggered off to the shower with a chocolate covered toddler tucked under her arm, muttering about Tom's very apt choice of music.

By twelve o' clock they were all set to go. Everyone was showered and smartly dressed, the table had been carried through to the sitting room and fully extended, with an extra table of the same height added on so there was now room for everyone, and then it had been set by Jade with her usual artistic flair and looked quite stunning.

Within ten minutes the rest of the family had arrived, Kate and Sam with their two little ones, followed by Grandad and Joe, who had arrived the previous day to stay for a week with his dad. Their brother looked slightly harassed, having had to organise Grandad without making him feel he was being rushed as this might have caused the old man to dig his heels in and go even more slowly, which hadn't worked at all.

"Had to have his 20 minute shower, then his Weetabix, then his morning stroll" explained Joe, "I was ready to give him a fireman's lift just to get him into the bloody car."

"Don't fret about it" said Annie "he'll be happy now that he knows he's wound you up enough."

Harry and Nancy appeared shortly after, bringing the promised shortbread as well as a raspberry cheesecake and a very large, scrumptious looking Pavlova.

"They look amazing" said Annie "we'll have at least six choices of dessert now."

"I'll write out a pudding menu" Jade offered "I can use my new calligraphy set and it'll save us having to tell Grandad at least three times when he mishears us."

Dinner was served at 2pm on the dot, the centre of the long table crammed with serving dishes full of vegetables and the ceremony began when Tom brought the turkey through on a huge platter, surrounded by pigs in blankets and whole roasted chestnuts.

They all pulled crackers, put on their paper hats and read out the terrible jokes while Tom started carving and when all their plates were piled high they said grace and then tucked in with great gusto, laughing and chatting throughout the meal which lasted the better part of an hour. Even Grandad was in fine form, having had a couple of sherries and Kate had also managed to turn his hearing aid off, using the excuse that she was just changing the battery, for which he thanked her and said he could hear much better now.

When everyone was finally finished they took a break as the table was cleared, wine glasses replenished and the dessert menu pored over while they tried a short table quiz.

"What's the name of the female lead character in My Fair Lady" asked Tom.

"Eliza Doolittle" said Kate.

"No, that's the one who talks to animals" said Grandad "but he's a bloke."

"That's Doctor Doolittle" said Tom.

"Doctor who?" asked Lee.

"Not him, you daftie" snorted Grandad "he's the one who lives in a police box and fights The Garlics."

"Let's have another question" said Joe.

"OK, what's the capital of Paraguay?"

"Ascuncion" answered Nancy.

"Bless you" said Grandad.

"My brain hurts" Tom groaned.

"Time for pudding" announced Jade.

The afternoon was very relaxed. Once the tables had been cleared and the furniture put back in place they watched the younger ones playing Twister then had a game of Charades and eventually put a light hearted film on the telly while the adults took turns to have a snooze, so it was eight o' clock that night before everyone began to make a move homewards. Kate and her crew were the first to leave, followed closely by Joe and his dad. Grandad was still wearing his paper hat, set at a rakish angle, and a tinsel boa round his neck. He was unaware that Jade had also pinned several glittery baubles in a neat line down the back of his coat.

"Wish you hadn't done that" moaned Joe "I was hoping to go to the pub for an hour."

"Just take him home first" said Annie "he's absolutely knackered so make him a cup of Horlicks and he'll be asleep before it's finished."

"If you hang his coat up backwards he might not notice the baubles when he goes for his paper in the morning." said Tom

"I'd pay good money to see that." Harry laughed as he walked out to the car with them and Nancy said their farewells,

"We've had the most fantastic day" said Nancy "I can't remember the last time I laughed so much."

"My mum always used to say it was the best medicine in the world" said Annie "which is probably why we spend so much time doing it."

"I envy you that, you just always seem to see the funny side of things, no matter what."

"Oh, it's not always easy" Annie replied "but it helps to see the up-side when you can."

Nancy smiled,

"That's called PMA, Positive Mental Attitude" she said.

"Well, it beats the hell out of PMT any time" retorted Annie.

CHAPTER TWENTY FOUR

It was only the third Monday of the New Year and Annie was already suffering a bad case of the January blues.

The children were back at school, Tom back to work and Aunt Lizzie was away for a fortnight, visiting an old friend, whilst Harry and Nancy had taken themselves off to Italy for a second honeymoon. To cap it all, Kate was on night duty for a week at the local hospital which meant she wasn't available during the daytime, so Annie had no-one to moan to at all.

Her only companion today was Rory but, as much as she loved him dearly, his conversational skills were still sadly lacking.

This morning nothing had gone right, beginning with a mad scramble when the alarm clock didn't go off, Tom blaming her for not setting it properly, Jade and Lee not being able to find gym kits or homework jotters and both still bickering at each other as they raced out the door for the school bus.

When they'd all gone Annie had gazed round the kitchen, where it looked as though a bomb had been dropped, and realised with a sinking heart that the pile of dishes overflowing the sink were hers and hers alone, because Aunt Lizzie wasn't there to be fairy godmother this time.

It had taken her over an hour to clean up the mess then she'd put Rory down for his nap and spent half an hour splitting logs, a task that she and Tom shared and that she usually enjoyed as it gave her a chance to let off steam. This morning, however, she'd been a bit too enthusiastic with the axe and a large chunk of wood had flown off and cracked her on the shin, and then she'd discovered the kindling was lying in a puddle in the back of the leaky coal shed.

After that the fire had taken ages to light and was also belching smoke because, despite the endless lists Annie had made before Christmas, she had forgotten to put 'sweep chimney' on any of them.

The utility room and bathroom were festooned with lines of wet washing because the tumble drier had finally given up the ghost and this only added to the ongoing problem they had with dampness where Annie was constantly re-sticking bits of peeling wallpaper and wiping off patches of mould in both rooms.

"I hate January" she muttered to herself as she washed the shelves in the food cupboards "I bloody well hate it."

She had put all the tins on the floor for Rory to play with and he was having a grand old time building them up as high as he could then cackling with delight when they eventually toppled over with a crash.

The tins were getting seriously dented but Annie could not have cared less.

Sophie had picked up on her mood as well and was wandering about forlornly with a pathetic, droopy expression on her big, dopey face.

A short time later Annie had her head and shoulders in the depths of the second cupboard, working on the top shelf and peering warily into tins that contained festering mince pies and fermenting Christmas cake when she heard and felt an ominous rumble.

Annie knew exactly what to expect when she opened the sitting room door and she was right.

There had been a fall of soot from the chimney that had completely smothered the fire and was spilling over into the fireplace and a cloud of dense, stinking coal dust hovered in the air for a moment before drifting slowly down to cover every single surface in the room, as well as clinging to the walls and curtains.

She was standing there in the middle of it all, wondering if the house insurance was up to date so that she could put a match to the whole bloody lot of it when Rory toddled through, gave a couple of little coughs and handed her a bundle of tin labels.

She picked him up, cuddled him as hard as she dared, then went to sit in the kitchen with him while she had a damn good cry.

When Jade and Lee came in from school their mum refused to let them into the sitting room, dished up meatballs and spaghetti hoops, followed by prunes and tapioca for their tea, leaving a number of other opened cans on the draining board, and Sophie had a cardboard sign round her neck that proclaimed 'the end of the world is nigh' in huge black letters.

Tom came home shortly afterwards, got the children upstairs via the front door and took Annie through to their bedroom where he brought her a bottle of wine and a glass, then got to work with buckets of hot, soapy water.

Several hours later he had done as much as he could, so he ran the gauntlet of wet washing in the bathroom to have a shower.

The final straw came when he stepped out and was immediately cocooned by an entire strip of wallpaper that had finally lost its grip on the streaming walls.

Eventually he climbed into bed and snuggled up beside Annie who sniffed loudly and announced,

"I've run out of PMA."

Tom gave her a hug and replied,

"Sod this for a game of soldiers, let's go and see mum this weekend."

Jade and Lee could not believe their luck when they heard they were having extra time off school so soon after going back, but they realised their mum was seriously stressed out so they showed their appreciation by helping as much as they could round the house for the next few days.

Annie called in a professional chimney sweep, sent the curtains to the cleaners, hired a machine to shampoo the carpets and upholstery, and the walls and furniture were scrubbed twice, with help from Kate now that she was finished night shifts.

By the time they all piled into the car on Thursday evening Annie was already feeling much better, Grandad having offered to pet sit while they were away since Aunt Lizzie wasn't due home for another week.

Tom was dubious about this as they drove up the lane and wondered if it was really a good idea.

"Don't fret yourself" Annie said cheerfully "Kate will be checking in now and then – he'll be fine."

"Either that or he'll be in a straitjacket" Tom remarked ominously.

CHAPTER TWENTY FIVE

The trip down was speedy and peaceful because it was overnight, the motorway wasn't at all busy and the children slept most of the way.

However, although Annie liked to try and stay awake to keep Tom company, she got bored sitting still for so long and ate constantly, while her husband fretted about the mess she was making in his car with the picnic.

This was a bone of contention on every trip because Annie insisted on having the food boxes piled around her feet, rather than in the boot as Tom would prefer, when it could only be eaten if they stopped and got out of the car.

After his third sarcastic comment Annie had had enough.

"Oh, for Pete's sake it's only a few crumbs" she snapped "I'll get your mum's hoover out in the morning."

"Annie, you've never cleaned a car in your life, inside or out."

His wife bristled but knew she couldn't argue on that point.

"It's only a bloody car Tom, not the Hilton."

"But I keep telling you it's also my office at times – and there's nothing worse than reaching into the glove box for a pen and sticking my fingers in an old jam doughnut."

A silence descended in the car for ten minutes or so until Tom sighed heavily and said,

"Oh, what's the point, go on then."

There was a frantic rustling in the dark until Annie found a bag of crisps and a packet of Penguins, then a click and a hiss as she opened a fizzy drink.

For the next few minutes there was only the sound of munching and an occasional burp until Annie whispered,

"They wouldn't be jam doughnuts anyway, I only like the custard ones."

They arrived at Ellen and Mary's just after five in the morning and after hugs had been exchanged Jade and Lee staggered off to their beds while the rest of them drank tea and caught up with all the family news and Rory slept on in his car seat.

"We've got a lot to fit in to your three days" said Ellen "thought we'd have a picnic in the park this afternoon, maybe a few hours at the beach tomorrow then a family meal and games in the evening. Haven't thought about Sunday yet though, any ideas?"

Annie was on her way out of the room at this point,

"A few hours of doing nothing would be nice" she said caustically.

The others ignored her remark and continued chatting for a while until Tom started yawning,

"Right" said his mum "get yourself off to bed, I won't be going back now so I can see to Rory, that's if he ever wakes up"

They looked to where Rory was still sleeping soundly on the sofa and Tom laughed,

"Doubt if he'll wake before eight, he likes his ten hours sleep, just like the other two."

"Wish you could say the same about that daft wife of yours, can't you take her with you before we fall out with the neighbours?" said Mary.

"Why, what's she done now" asked Tom.

"She's outside Dustbusting that bloody car of yours."

After a few hours of sleep Ellen announced that they would take lunch to the park in the form of hot sausage and bacon rolls wrapped in foil and flasks of soup, coffee and hot chocolate.

"We're meeting up with Linda and her lot so we can take frisbees and a football" she said.

Annie was not pleased.

"It's piggin' freezing out there and blowing a gale" she protested.

"Nonsense" said Ellen "it will clear the cobwebs and we'll all feel the better for it."

"But I don't want to go" Annie whined "I just want to curl up by the fire and read my book."

Ellen was not to be messed with,

"Honestly, I thought you country folk were hardy creatures, used to all weathers and tougher than us townies" she sniffed.

"I am tough as a rule" said Annie "but I'm on holiday and I'd rather be looking at the weather from the inside today."

"Your coat and wellies are by the back door and everyone else is ready" said Ellen, and that was the end of the discussion.

In the wide open expanse of the park the wind was fiercer than ever and there was a definite hint of rain in the air but no-one except Annie seemed to notice or care.

Tom and Phil joined in with the five youngsters and spent half an hour racing round the park kicking a football as well as trying vainly to get a couple of kites airborne, while the women took a brisk walk through the woods then dragged a couple of picnic benches together and set out the food.

The soup and rolls disappeared in record time then the young ones were all for a game of frisbee, so they went charging off again.

"This is insane," Annie moaned "we could all be nice and cosy round the fire right now."

"Oh, for Pete's sake girl, just shut up and have a banana" laughed Ellen, shoving the said piece of fruit into Annie's hand.

Annie took it and sat munching miserably for a few minutes.

"If I threw a tantrum would you make me go and sit in the car?" she asked eventually, then she was pelted with the stale bread that had been brought to feed the ducks and Mary said,

"If you don't cheer up, we'll tie you to the roof rack for the journey home."

A short time later the children retrieved the bread and went to feed the ducks while the adults talked about how they dealt with the January blues.

"I just write and eat wine gums" said Annie.

"I spend money I haven't got" Linda chipped in.

"You and a few million others, I should think" said Mary "I like to decorate, freshen up the house for springtime."

"And you like to move furniture, don't you mum?" said Tom, grinning slyly.

Ellen looked at him suspiciously.

"Well, yes I do, there's nothing better after Mary has finished painting than to move a few things round – makes the place feel almost like a new home" she admitted "I've done it every year since you were all small."

Tom and his sister both snorted at the same time.

"Oh, we remember that well, don't we sis, how mum used to move the furniture round?"

"But without telling us in advance" his sister backed him up.

Ellen shifted uncomfortably and suggested it was time to pack up, but Annie wanted revenge and insisted they hear the classic story once more.

"Go on then Linda" she said, enjoying Ellen's blushes "remind us again about how you ended up in casualty because of your mum."

At that point the children had just returned and were intrigued.

"How did that happen?" asked Jade.

Linda then went on to relate the story of when she had just turned eighteen and had gone out with friends after work for a few drinks.

"It was only supposed to be for a couple of hours, but it was nearly midnight when I got home so I'd had a few more drinks than I'd intended."

"So, what happened then" prompted Annie.

"Well, I was trying to be really quiet, crept up the stairs without waking anyone – then I went to throw myself onto where my bed used to be and bounced off the wardrobe instead – a broken nose and two black eyes, thanks to mum."

Shortly afterwards it began to rain heavily so Annie grabbed Rory and was the first one back to the car, leaving the others to gather up children, toys and picnic remains and when they got home they trooped up the back garden path to strip off all their wet and muddy coats and boots in the porch.

Tom was struggling with his wellies, which were really old and perished round the ankles and had let in water.

"I think my socks have swollen," he said "give me a hand here, Annie"

His wife grabbed hold of one foot with her back towards Tom and pulled, while he put his other foot on her backside and pushed as hard as he could.

Several minutes later Annie was still heaving and muttering and Tom was still pushing with all of his might when there was a sudden ripping sound as the foot parted company with the rest of the wellie.

At this point Tom was left wearing a vulcanised leg warmer while his wife shot off down the path like an Exocet missile, tripped over a rubbish sack and landed, spread-eagled, in the muddiest part of the garden.

By the time Annie got back to the house and stripped off her outdoor gear there wasn't a soul to be seen but she could hear muffled noises from behind several doors as she stomped up the stairs and locked herself in the bathroom for an hour.

The rest of the day was very lazy and they spent the evening playing Monopoly without a single reference to Annie's spectacular sprint and dive, although there were a few twitchy lips from time to time.

However, when it was time for the older children to go to bed Lee just couldn't resist a parting shot as he left the room,

"Nice landing there, mum – ever thought of joining the circus and being fired from a cannon?"

He quickly shut the door behind him, just as Annie threw her slipper in that direction and the rest of them finally dissolved into full blown hysterics.

The remaining time passed quickly with the seaside trip that Annie categorically refused to go on, a mad family games night and on the final day a huge Sunday dinner for all the family.

On this occasion Annie had insisted on cooking the meal while the others were at church because she thought it would be a novelty to use appliances that didn't need seven bells knocked out of them to make them work.

The resulting dinner had a great deal of entertainment value as well because Annie had never mastered using a gas cooker so her gravy was lumpy, the bread sauce could be cut into slices and the roast potatoes and parsnips were so crisp they could not be cut without a considerable struggle. This caused Rory endless amusement as he watched them all ducking to avoid flying shrapnel and he thought it was all a great game, so he joined in the fun by using his trifle as a frisbee and his dad ended up wearing a jelly and custard wig.

They left at tea-time, having had their humour batteries well and truly recharged and feeling able to cope with anything, which just as well as they had Grandad and Cinders waiting to welcome them home.

CHAPTER TWENTY SIX

Grandad had survived his pet-sitting duties but there was a distinct note of relief in his voice when he handed over again at ten o' clock that night.

"I reckon they were all conspiring against me" he complained "between Cinders scaring Sophie half to death a few times, her moping about and going off her food, then the two of them getting rid of it from one end or the other as soon as my back was turned, it's been a bloody nightmare."

Annie sympathised with him over a cup of tea while Tom put Rory to bed and Jade and Lee got their school stuff organised for the morning.

Sophie's joy knew no bounds at the sight of them, the rabbit practically went into spasm and even Cinders looked as though she was trying for a lop-sided smile, but Tom reckoned it was either a sneer or she was suffering from wind.

Annie was also thrilled to see that her dad had given the sitting room and hall a fresh coat of paint, so the house looked even better than when they left and she was truly glad to be home.

After Tom had taken Grandad home they were all heading for bed when Annie announced,

"I feel completely relaxed and inspired now" she said, "and tomorrow I'll start a new list just so we can keep things on top of things and everyone does their share ...."

She stopped when she realised there was no thunderous applause and when she turned round the kitchen was empty.

Next morning Annie rose in high spirits, driving the rest of them mad by talking incessantly, singing along to the radio and dancing round the table as she served breakfast.

The only one who seemed to appreciate her mood was Rory, who drummed along in his high chair with his spoon, occasionally flicking Weetabix and singing along with his mum.

Tom, Jade and Lee couldn't get themselves out of the house quickly enough and they all got stuck in the back doorway as they tried to exit at the same time.

Lee was in the middle of the trio and after a bit of a struggle he was popped out into the garden like a cork from a bottle.

"Good grief, dad" said Jade "how are we going to survive this?"

"I don't know, honey" Tom replied "but we'll have to think of something drastic if she keeps this up, maybe I could get my hands on some Valium and slip it into her morning cuppa."

Alone at last with Rory, Annie continued to sparkle her way through the chores. She went through the kitchen and bathroom like a whirling dervish while he toddled along behind her and put sticky little fingerprints on everything she'd cleaned.

She hoovered and dusted the sitting room and made a spectacular dried flower arrangement for the coffee table, then when she took Rory for his nap she stripped and remade all the beds.

Just as she was putting the last pillowcase on she heard a car pull into the farmyard and looked out to see Aunt Lizzie climbing out of a taxi.

Before the old lady's bags had even been unloaded her niece was upon her.

"It's so good to have you home, Aunt Lizzie" Annie cried "you will never know how much we've missed you."

Aunt Lizzie's voice was muffled in Annie's bear hug, but when she was finally released she beamed with pleasure.

"I'll have to go away more often, if this is the welcome I get."

Annie took her bags from the smiling taxi driver and they went into the kitchen, with Annie talking nineteen to the dozen.

"Slow down child, sounds like you've been inhaling cleaning fluids - I can't understand a word you're saying."

"Sorry Aunt Lizzie, I'm just so happy to see you – we weren't expecting you till Friday."

"Well, I wanted to surprise you, which is why I didn't phone, but to be honest I was ready to come home after the first three days"

She went on to explain that she'd spent a very tedious ten days with her friend who had done nothing but moan about life in general and complain about her aches and pains.

"Honestly Annie, she just sounded so *old.*"

Her niece had to smile because she knew the lady in question was at least five years Lizzie's junior.

"What scares me most is that if I still lived near her, I'd probably be the same by now."

"No chance Aunt Lizzie, you'll always be young at heart."

"Well, it must be living here with you mad lot that does it."

Several hours later the women had finally caught up on their news and Aunt Lizzie had been moved to tears when Rory woke up and was so delighted to see her that he threw his chubby little arms round her neck and gave her a big slobbery kiss.

She walked up the lane with him to meet Jade and Lee off the school bus and was nearly knocked off her feet when they saw her.

Grandad called in for a cuppa shortly after and even he was obviously glad to see her because he gave her a quick awkward hug and a peck on the forehead.

When Tom came home from work he lifted the old lady off her feet and swung her round till she was dizzy, then gave her a great big kiss on the cheek.

"Thank God you're home" he whispered "the family is complete again and you can keep an eye on that mad bloody woman of mine so we can all sleep safely in our beds once more"

Aunt Lizzie's response was to sit down heavily on a chair and burst into tears.

"That's it," she sniffed eventually "I can't be doing with this crying lark so I'm never, ever going to go away again."

CHAPTER TWENTY SEVEN

Several weeks later it was Annie's birthday and she was woken with tea and toast in bed and a pile of cards and presents.

After opening and admiring the sun clock and the trowel that Jade and Lee had made for her at school and the box of wine gums from Rory, she was completely gobsmacked to discover her next present was a laptop computer – a joint gift from Tom, Aunt Lizzie and Grandad.

"This is absolutely fantastic" she beamed "now I'll be able to write anywhere I like."

"I've also set you up with an email address, whether you like it or not, it will take five minutes to show you how to use it, right after breakfast" her husband said firmly

"You can work out in the garden, in the greenhouse or down by the river." said Aunt Lizzie

"Even in the pub." said Tom caustically

"Now that's a brilliant idea" said Annie, ignoring the sarcasm "imagine the ideas for chapters I could get from some of the characters who drink there."

"Good grief, Tom" said the old lady sternly "now you've just given her license to sit in the pub every day."

"Like she wouldn't have thought of it herself eventually" he replied.

Annie spent most of the morning experimenting with her new toy and drove the family mad by sending them emails from every room in the house, via Tom's tablet.

'I'm in the utility room sorting out the laundry - lots of snotty hankies and grotty single socks – thanks for that Tom and Lee.'

Sitting room - 'Just about to light the fire – need you to fill coal bucket and bring in more logs Tom, ta very much.'

Kitchen - 'I'm out tonight so dinner will be served whenever someone decides to cook and dish it up.'

'Jade, seriously girl, that is one ugly guy on that poster – looks like a bulldog chewing a wasp.'

'Tell Lee to get his butt up here now - and bring some disinfectant!'

There was a furtive gathering later in the afternoon,

"We've created a monster" moaned Tom "how long will she keep this up?"

"No, *you* created the monster, showing her how to email in the first place" scolded Aunt Lizzie.

"I've had an idea" said Lee.

"Did it hurt" asked his sister, scathingly.

Her brother ignored her and continued,

"She doesn't need the internet to do her writing" he reminded them "all we have to do is get her to work in the caravan and she'll be out of Broadband range so she can't pester us with emails, and she hates texting so she won't do that either."

His dad and Aunt Lizzie looked at him in admiration, even Jade was grudgingly impressed,

"I'll go and start jazzing it up now, make it really nice and comfy" she said.

"You're a genius, child" Aunt Lizzie said to Lee.

"I know" he grinned.

An hour later they led Annie to the caravan and when she saw all the lovely cushions and drapes Jade had spread around, as well as posters and framed photos of the family, a vase of flowers and the big flask of coffee and box of posh biscuits she was in raptures.

"This is amazing" she said "it's a perfect office, nice and cosy with the gas fire on and plenty of light – I'll get my laptop now and have an hour or two in here I think."

"That sounds like a plan" said Tom, and they watched as Annie dashed across the lawn, while Lee just enjoyed being the hero of the moment.

Early that evening there was a make-over session while they all got ready to go to the pub for a ladies' night that happened to coincide with Annie's birthday. On this occasion Jade opted not to bring out the wax strips or tweezers, having been threatened by her mum that she would not be allowed to go with them if she did, so they settled for face masks and manicures instead.

Nancy was also there, this being her first pub night out with them, and she enjoyed the banter that went on as they painted their nails, applied their masks and kept their wine glasses topped up.

After her glass had been filled for the third time though, Nancy had to protest,

"I need to slow down" she said "I just haven't got your stamina yet, I won't even make it to the pub if I carry on like this."

Tom was passing through at that moment, on his way to have a bath.

"Not to worry Nancy" he remarked "you'll soon get the hang of it – especially if you're going to a ladies' night with this bunch – baptism by fire I think it's known as."

Nancy paled slightly, then took a hefty swig of wine,

"Might as well start practising" she announced.

Ten minutes later Kate groaned.

"I need to pee" she said "Tom's going to be ages yet though, isn't he?"

"Yup" said Annie "never takes less than an hour when he has his weekly bath."

"It's about time you had a second toilet put in" her sister complained,

"That would be good," Nancy grinned "then you could call the house 'Lautrec' - cos it would have two loos."

"I'm very much liking your sense of humour" said Annie "I need to write that one down."

Unbeknown to her sister, Kate had also contacted a number of other friends who might not normally be there and invited them to turn up as a surprise, so there were about twenty in their group by the time everyone arrived and Annie was really chuffed to see them all.

As usual they put a load of tunes on the juke box and there were piles of coins round the pool table, so they started the evening playing a few friendly games, while those who didn't want to just sat chatting or dancing round their handbags.

One topic of conversation was about the fact that some of their children were now studying for exams and the resultant stress and mood swings that the rest of the family were having to put up with because of it.

"We're walking on eggshells most of the time" said one of the mums "we never know if it's going to be Pollyanna or Miss Trunchbull who comes down the stairs in the mornings."

"Huh, you want to try living with The Grinch" said the mother of a fourteen-year old boy.

Another mum, Sarah, was not to be outdone,

"We've been there with two of them and survived – but now that Jill is in her second year at Uni and Pete starts as well after the summer, the strain is all on our bank account."

"Changed days," said one of the older mums "I remember when we finished school, got a job and moved out – and sometimes even sent money home to our parents."

"Unfortunately, that's not how it's done these days" ventured another "we're supposed to be there as their financial cushion till they're into their twenties at least."

"I know" Sarah groaned "but nobody warns you that the bloody cushion is the size of a bouncy castle."

At nine o' clock the pool table cover was put on then all the dishes of food that everyone had brought were spread out and, while they were eating, the participating teams pored over the music quiz and filled in their answers.

Annie's team were doing well as they had a good age range with Aunt Lizzie to cover the 50's and 60's era at one end and Jade's knowledge on the more recent stuff, while the others filled the gaps in between.

"Right" said Kate "this next one is six songs and the artists all have colours in their name, one point for each or ten points if we get them all. First one is Breakfast at Tiffany's."

"Audrey Hepburn" said Aunt Lizzie "but that doesn't have a colour in it."

"That's the film, we're talking about the song."

"It's Deep Blue Something" said Nancy.

"Yes, but what's the something." asked Aunt Lizzie.

"That *is* the band's name" explained Kate, her aunt looked baffled but just shrugged.

"Next one – American Idiot."

"Green Day" said Jade.

"Fairground?"

"Simply Red." Annie offered, as her sister filled in the answers.

"Moves like Jagger."

"Maroon 5" said Jade.

"I Gotta Feeling."

"Black Eyed Peas" said Nancy and Kate at the same time.

"We're doing well here" said Kate "just one more to go and we'll get the bonus."

"Bloody silly names" sniffed Aunt Lizzie.

"Well, the last one is 60's so that's your era – who sang 'Mirror, Mirror'?

The old lady had the grace to blush.

"That would be Pinkerton's Assorted Colours" she mumbled.

"Not a daft name at all" said Kate as the others laughed,

No-one else had known that answer so they won the quiz by four points which they all agreed was thanks to Aunt Lizzie and that cheered her up no end.

The final part of the evening was the karaoke which none of them were brave enough to try until they'd seen half a dozen really dire attempts and then Sarah, having had a few more than her usual glasses of wine, launched herself onto the stage and grabbed the microphone, belted out a mixture of lyrics from several different songs and then sat back down at their table to a rather muted applause.

"Well done Sarah" said Aunt Lizzie "that was a very brave attempt."

Sarah looked at them all with a bleary expression on her face,

"So, what was wrong with it" she slurred.

Kate leaned forward and said quietly,

"It's just that we've never heard the song about the gypsy woman who wanted to go home on the country roads to stand by her man."

If she had been capable of glaring, Sarah would have done so, instead she muttered,

"The trouble with you lot, is that you've got no soul" before putting her head down on the table and falling into a sound sleep.

Tom and Harry arrived at midnight, just as Sarah was being helped into a car by her husband, protesting loudly to some of the others who were waiting outside,

"It wasn't my fault" she was pleading "you saw what happened, didn't you?"

Annie answered her husband's questioning look,

"Some silly bugger woke her up by ringing a bell right by her ear" she explained "she gave him a bloody nose."

Aunt Lizzie was highly amused,

"Hope the poor lass isn't barred for it" she chuckled "but that was a punch Rocky Marciano would have been proud of."

CHAPTER TWENTY EIGHT

Annie was hoovering in the hall one evening when her dad came through to say he was heading home because it was getting dark and his bike lights weren't too clever.

She continued to hoover as they talked because it made no difference to the volume of their conversation.

"I think they need new batteries" he shouted "but I've brought this, just in case."

So saying he pulled a torch out of his pocket.

"You're not going to cycle home one-handed, are you?" yelled Annie.

Her dad looked at her as if she had horns growing out of her head.

"Don't be so bloody daft" he scoffed "it fits in my hat."

As she watched in disbelief he produced a toy policeman's helmet that had been abandoned by Lee years ago.

He had cut a small round hole in the front of it which he jammed the torch into then he put it triumphantly on his head, held in place by a huge elastic band under his chin.

At that moment Aunt Lizzie passed by with barely a glance at them and announced over the din that she was going to heat some soup.

Annie was transfixed at the sight of her dad with a tiny helmet perched on his head while he demonstrated his new toy and proudly switched the torch on and off a few times.

She had just about found her voice to make a comment when the house was suddenly plunged into darkness and the hoover was silenced.

In the distance Aunt Lizzie could be heard shouting,

"Sorry – I turned on the wrong piggin' ring on the cooker."

Annie was aware of her dad standing beside her and the next second she was blinded by his torch shining straight into her eyes.

"Give me that thing, you silly old sod" she said, as she reached up to pull the hat off and heard him curse when she accidentally twanged the elastic band against his throat.

She used the torch to find her way into the cupboard under the stairs where she then pushed the mains switch back to the 'on' position.

As she did so the lights came on and the hoover roared back into life, right beside her dad, causing him to hold on to the banister for a few minutes till his heart rate slowed down again.

A week later Annie drove down the lane into the farmyard just as a large van was leaving and when she got out of the car the whole family were hovering at the back door, apparently waiting for her.

"What's up?" she asked "you're all looking decidedly furtive."

"There's a surprise for you in the kitchen" said Lee with a grin.

His mum peered through the door suspiciously.

"You have to go right in" said Jade "it's at the other end."

Annie moved further into the L-shaped room and glanced round the corner cautiously.

"Bloody hell!" she exclaimed, taking a quick step backward and treading on Tom's foot as she did so.

Her husband pulled a face, let out a quiet moan and managed not to swear.

"Well, what do you think?" asked Aunt Lizzie impatiently

Annie walked properly into the kitchen and stared hard at the brand new white, black and chrome cooker with a ceramic hob and after a moment or two she announced,

"It's a bit shiny isn't it?"

"Told you she wouldn't be impressed" Aunt Lizzie sniffed.

"But there's a nice new set of saucepans for you as well" Lee piped up, then realised his mistake when he got a dig in the ribs from Jade.

His mum turned on him with a withering stare,

"Do these saucepans have *my* name engraved on them, pray tell?"

"Sorry mum, I meant *we* got new saucepans" said Lee.

"Well, I hope you and your saucepans will be very happy together" his mum retorted.

"Aw, mum, don't be so horrible" scolded Jade "aren't you pleased at all?"

Annie relented at last and smiled,

"Yes, of course I am, it's a lovely surprise – it's just a bit shiny, that's all."

Aunt Lizzie sniggered,

"It won't be like that for long, I dare say."

Annie turned to glare at them all,

"Oh, yes it bloody will' she replied "it's the first brand new cooker we've ever had so it had *better* be looked after."

Tom took the children into town that afternoon and when they returned he produced a few brown paper bags containing Chinese take-away.

"Thought it would save a lot of hassle" he explained "I knew Aunt Lizzie was at her darts club and that you'd probably be writing all afternoon."

The next day Annie also had to go into town to pick up more ink cartridges and paper for her printer, so she treated the family to pizzas for dinner.

The following night Aunt Lizzie took the family for a meal in the local hotel to celebrate a small win on the lottery and the night after that Jade and Lee were staying over with friends, so the grown-ups phoned for an Indian take-away.

During that night Annie got up to go to the loo and was startled to find Tom and Aunt Lizzie standing in the darkness of the kitchen, just staring at the cooker with its luminous clock and dials that appeared to be winking at them.

Tom finally said what they'd all been thinking for days,

"This is ridiculous" he whispered "someone has to be brave enough to try the thing out or these piggin' take-aways will end up costing us more than it was to buy it in the first place."

CHAPTER TWENTY NINE

A few weeks later the conversation at the breakfast table centred around Jade's forthcoming mock exams and her need to make her subject choices for the following year. Not surprisingly she was very keen on the artistic options as she was fairly sure she'd like to work in a job such as interior design or similar.

"I have to do English obviously and I'll definitely need art and craft and design" she said as she looked over the list she'd been given at school,

"What about a language?" asked her dad

"Yeah, I was thinking about that, I reckon French would be best."

"I'm going to choose languages when it's my turn" Lee chipped in.

His sister turned on him with any icy stare.

"You've barely mastered English, you wally"

Aunt Lizzie tutted and shook her head at Jade.

"Give him a break girl" she remonstrated, then turned to Lee, "and what other kind of subjects would you choose?"

"I'm not sure what else I'll need" he replied.

"Well, a brain would be helpful for a start" sneered Jade.

"Stop being so horrible" Annie interrupted "we've heard your choices, now let Lee speak."

"I'm going to work for the government and be a spy" he announced, then glared at his sister as she choked and sprayed orange juice into her cereal.

Tom kept his expression completely neutral as he said,

"Well, languages would be handy right enough, but you'll need maths and sciences for definite."

"I don't like maths."

"But you'll need it to work out algorithms and crack codes."

Lee was looking a lot less certain now,

"Maybe I'll just be a detective then."

Jade snorted again,

"You can't even find a pair of matching socks….." she began,

"Ok, that's enough, let's continue this discussion another time" Tom announced firmly.

Later that morning Annie was at her desk when she heard a commotion from upstairs but decided to ignore it, knowing she'd be dragged into it soon enough.

Five minutes later Jade barged into the room, fizzing with rage.

"Mum, have you got any Blue Tac?" she demanded.

"I have indeed" replied Annie.

"Well, can I have some then?"

"Tut, tut child, where are your manners?"

Jade glared at her while her mum gazed steadily back then she finally took a deep breath and said slowly,

"Can I have some Blue Tac – *please?*"

"Of course you can dear" said Annie, opening her top drawer "would this have anything to do with the ruckus I just heard?"

"Lee has been in my room and pinched mine – I know he has, but he won't admit it."

Annie pulled a fair sized lump off her supply and handed it to her daughter.

"There you are sweetheart, and don't use it all at once."

She could tell that Jade was making a superhuman effort to restrain herself, but she managed a muttered 'thanks' before charging out of the room.

Annie looked at her watch and started to count down.

It took just four minutes for Lee to appear, looking sheepish.

"Mum, have you got any tweezers?" he asked.

Whatever Annie had been expecting, it wasn't that so she just stared at him, eyebrows raised.

Lee shuffled uncomfortably,

"Well, it was Jade's fault really – she just came crashing into my room shouting about the Blue Tac."

Annie continued to stare, until he grudgingly admitted,

"I didn't have time to hide it anywhere, so I shoved it in my ear and now it's stuck."

The resultant noise from the study caused Tom to stick his head round the door and when Annie was finally capable of explaining he couldn't help but join in the laughter, even Lee could see the funny side of it now.

However, before leaving the room he made his parents solemnly swear that they would never tell Jade,

"It would be all over school tomorrow" he said pleadingly "I'd have to join the Foreign Legion."

After he left Tom looked at Annie and shook his head slowly.

"If he hadn't given up the idea of working for the government, I shudder to think that he might one day have been involved in our nation's security."

CHAPTER THIRTY

On the morning of Lee's eleventh birthday the family gathered round the breakfast table to watch him open his presents.

As always, he grabbed the biggest one first, the label saying it was from Aunt Lizzie. He ripped off the paper, opened the box and found a smaller one inside which he took out and opened to find a smaller one still, and so it went on until he opened the final one to find a pack of seven pairs of socks.

Luckily, he appreciated the humour and grinned at the old lady

"Thanks Aunt Lizzie, they're great."

"They've got the days of the week on them," she pointed out "so mind you change them every day cos I'll be checking."

"Well, at least he'll know what day of the week it is" Jade chipped in "he needs all the help he can get with that."

"Ah, but what if he wears odd ones" said Annie "what will happen then?"

"It doesn't bear thinking about" said Tom.

It turned out that the smallest parcel was from his mum and dad and it was the digital camera he'd been hoping for.

"Excellent" he exclaimed "my own proper camera at last."

"I'll show you how to use it later" his dad offered "it's really simple though, even your mum could work it out."

"Bloody cheek" aid Annie

An hour or so later they all trooped out into the garden and lined up for some family photos, Tom hogging the camera at first, so that he could show Lee how it was done.

"But I know already, dad," Lee protested "I've used yours loads of times."

"Ah, but this is a different model so it will take some practise."

"Which is exactly what he wants to do now, Tom" said Annie.

"Can't you go and powder your nose or something," asked her husband, "it's a bit shiny."

"Piggin' charming," huffed Annie as she stamped indoors, to return a few minutes later with a white cardboard cone tied to her nose.

Only Tom was not amused.

"None of you are taking this seriously," he grumbled "there is a knack to it you know."

"Hell's teeth, Tom" his wife groaned "even I know you can take dozens of photos and delete all the crap ones, so who cares if they're not all perfect?"

Even Jade was impressed with her mum's apparent knowledge of digital cameras.

"Nice one, mum, you're finally catching up."

"Not really, it's just that the anorak salesman started his spiel by telling us that bit, I switched off before he got to the end of the sentence. Went for a burger and left them to it."

"He wasn't an anorak," Tom said defensively "just very knowledgeable."

Annie exhaled loudly,

"Remind me again how long you were in there?"

Tom looked uncomfortable,

"I suppose it was about an hour."

"There you go" said Annie "I rest my case."

Half an hour later they were still there and Lee hadn't yet managed to get his hands on the camera.

"For pity's sake Tom," Aunt Lizzie shouted at last "I'm losing the will to live here - get a move on before I pop my clogs."

"That can be arranged" muttered Tom.

Just at that point the phone rang indoors and there was a stampede to answer it, leaving just Rory, grinning happily at him.

"Ah well," he finally conceded "I suppose that's what they call a wrap."

Lee ran back to say the call was for Tom and could he *please* have his new camera now.

His dad handed it over at last with the parting shot,

"You can't use it straight away, you'll need to recharge the batteries first."

The following morning did not start well when Annie erupted volcanically at the state of the kitchen.

They'd had a special meal for Lee's birthday the night before, cooked by Tom and Jade and the kitchen was a shambles by the time they finished, but they'd promised to clean up afterwards.

Annie had gone through to the study later on for an hour or so and then straight to bed, so she wasn't aware it hadn't been done until she walked in on it next morning.

Her bellows of rage brought Tom, Jade and Aunt Lizzie scuttling into the kitchen.

"Get this bloody lot cleaned up NOW" she roared, and then as she saw Aunt Lizzie move towards the sink she yelled again,

"Don't you dare lift a finger Aunt Lizzie – you're not to wash so much as a teaspoon do you hear – you do it nearly every day and it's just not fair."

The old lady went into reverse and left the kitchen without a word.

Annie glared at the other two, picked up her laptop and cup of tea and stormed out of the door, marched across the lawn to the caravan and slammed the door behind her.

After taking a few deep breaths to calm herself, she opened her computer and began typing steadily, very soon lost in her work and completely oblivious to her surroundings.

Two hours and a few hundred words later, Annie decided it was time for some breakfast so she saved her work then got up to open the door.

This was when she discovered that it was jammed after she'd slammed it so hard and no amount of pushing, kicking or putting her shoulder to it would shift it.

Annie peered out of the windows but there was not a soul to be seen and, since the caravan was at the far end of the garden, she realised that shouting would be pointless.

Next she discovered that all the windows were stuck fast, either swollen by damp or rusted shut.

After struggling with them all and trying the door once more without success Annie could feel her temper rising again and decided on one final course of action.

She opened the door to the toilet where, thankfully, the window had still never been replaced, lifted her foot and kicked the hardboard pane with all of her might.

It took several attempts and twice her foot went through it and got stuck, leaving her hopping on the other foot and feeling quite foolish until she freed herself, thankful there was no-one around to witness her indignity.

Eventually though, she had kicked a hole big enough to allow her head and shoulders through, so she felt she could manage with that.

However, although she was successful in easing most of her body through, at the last moment her jumper caught on a jagged piece of hardboard and held fast.

The result was that Annie was left hanging upside down, with her legs still inside the caravan and wriggling like Houdini to try and get out of her jumper.

In the midst of this, and from her bat-like position, she caught a glimpse of Lee in the distance and gave a strangled yell to get his attention.

At that point her son disappeared, so she assumed he'd gone to get help.

Moments later she was aware of the whole family rushing across the grass, but they stopped within ten yards of her and collapsed onto the ground, laughing helplessly, while Lee took a few dozen photos with his new camera.

CHAPTER THIRTY ONE

A couple of weeks later the family had begun to notice that Annie was acting even more oddly than usual.

"She's been very secretive this last week or so" Aunt Lizzie announced one Saturday morning at breakfast with the rest of the family.

"I noticed that too" said Tom "she's not sleeping well and keeps leaping out of bed at all hours and disappearing with her laptop."

Lee frowned and then asked,

"What – like in a puff of smoke?"

Before Jade could physically harm her brother, Annie appeared, carrying a laundry basket of wet washing.

"Right – there's a pile of wood to be chopped for kindling and it's a nice day, so one of you can hang this lot out for me."

"I'll do the kindling" Jade offered quickly.

Annie dumped the basket on the floor and said,

"Don't care who does what – just get it done" then she left as quickly as she'd arrived.

"So that means I have to hang the washing out" said Lee.

"Sooner you than me if there are any of her knickers in there" his sister sniggered.

Lee's expression was one of horror.

"What do you mean?" he asked.

"Well, I'm not saying they're big" said his sister "but you could hoist them on poles and guide planes into Heathrow."

At this point Aunt Lizzie had to intervene,

"There's nothing wrong with what we used to call 'Harvest Festival' knickers" she protested.

Now Lee was baffled again and looked as though he was about to ask another question, while his sister covered her ears and groaned,

"I just know I don't want to hear this."

Tom simply looked at the older lady with raised eyebrows until she explained,

"All is safely gathered in."

Around mid-morning Jade announced that she was just going to walk down to the village to meet a friend for lunch.

"That's nice" said Annie "and I need to get a couple of parcels in the post, so I'll come with you."

"Not dressed like that you won't" said her daughter scathingly.

Annie looked down at herself,

"It's just jeans and a shirt" she said, "what's wrong with that?"

"I'm talking about the footwear" said Jade.

Annie sighed and rolled her eyes,

"Here we go again" she said resignedly.

It had long been a bone of contention between Annie and her daughter that her mum liked to wear Crocs, which Jade hated - so much so that she had managed to persuade the whole family to make jokes about them. In fact, that very morning Jade had sent Annie a post on Facebook with a picture of a pair of Crocs and the comment 'see those holes – that's where your dignity leaks out', which Annie had secretly thought was very funny but would never have admitted it.

"And that's your gardening shirt" Jade pointed out "you can change that as well."

"Oh, for Pete's sake, I'm only going to the village, not on the catwalk in Milan."

"Honestly mother" huffed Jade, on her way out of the door "if we were to be raided by the fashion police, you'd be well and truly nicked."

When Annie got back from the village Tom had still not returned from the shopping trip to town, having also taken Lee and Rory with him, so she disappeared into the study for ten minutes, then joined Aunt Lizzie in the garden for a coffee.

The old lady finally had to ask,

"Is everything ok, Annie?"

"What do you mean?" her niece responded.

"We've all noticed that you've been a bit distracted just lately, a bit quieter than your usual self as well."

Annie looked surprised.

"I didn't realise that – I thought I was acting pretty normally really."

"Now this is the point where we have to define what 'normal' is in this family" Aunt Lizzie laughed "and that could take a while!"

Just then they saw Tom's car coming down the lane, so Annie leaned over and squeezed her aunt's hand, smiling,

"I'm absolutely fine, honestly – all will be revealed soon enough."

When the car stopped Lee jumped out and headed straight for the house without saying anything, while Tom went round to liberate Rory from his car seat.

Annie's gaze followed Lee's disappearing form.

"Is there a problem?" she asked, to which her husband replied sharply,

"You could say that – and it's all your fault for asking me to get a bloody turnip."

He was referring to a farm on the way to town that left a wheelbarrow full of fresh vegetables at the bottom of the lane, customers took their choice and left the money in an honesty box.

Annie screwed up her face in puzzlement,

"But you've done that loads of times – what's the big deal today?"

Tom took a deep breath and continued,

"I was just slowing down and there was an old lady leaning over to get some carrots - then Lee opened his window and shouted "STOP – THIEF!'"

The two women were trying very hard to keep straight faces and, by now, so was Tom,

"Then what happened?" asked Aunt Lizzie.

"I just put my foot down and roared off – the last I saw in the rear-view mirror there were vegetables flying everywhere and she was running up the road like a bat out of hell."

Later that afternoon Tom came in from the garden sneezing violently and covered in grass, from mowing the lawn.

"I'm going for a shower" he gasped.

"Did you remember to buy soap?' asked his wife.

"No, I didn't, it wasn't on the list."

Annie rolled her eyes, pursed her lips and sighed,

"I think you'll find that it was" she replied.

Tom grabbed the jacket he'd been wearing to town and scanned the crumpled paper.

"Damn, so it was, I just missed it."

"There's still loads of those daft novelty soaps from Christmas" Aunt Lizzie suggested.

"Suppose they'll have to do then" Tom said grudgingly, heading for the bathroom.

He returned twenty minutes later saying the soap had been useless and wouldn't lather.

"Hardly surprising though" he continued "since it was a white chocolate golf ball."

CHAPTER THIRTY TWO

As soon as dinner was over that night Annie made her announcement.

"I've been asked to do an interview on the local radio, talking about my book, and someone wants to write an article about me."

After a moment or two of stunned silence there was a sudden clamour of surprised and delighted voices, all talking at once as they took turns to give her a hug. Rory was sitting on her lap and clapped his hands excitedly, even though he hadn't a clue what was going on.

"That's fantastic, Annie" Tom said, giving her a kiss.

"Well done lass, it's about time too" said Aunt Lizzie, beaming.

"That is so cool mum" was Jade's response.

"Will you get paid loads of money?" from Lee.

Annie laughed at her son.

"No, Lee, I don't get paid, but it is free publicity that will make a lot of people aware of the book, so hopefully it will help to sell a few copies once it's printed – although I'm going to start by publishing it online."

There was silence again for a minute while they all exchanged astonished looks, then Tom spoke again.

"I didn't even know you'd finished the book – and since when did you learn about online publishing?"

"OK, here's the thing – it's actually all down to Lee."

Lee sat up quickly, looking worried.

"Now what have I done?" he protested.

His mum laughed again and patted his arm.

"You haven't done anything wrong, honey – but remember when you asked me to help you with a poem for your homework a couple of months ago, and then your teacher asked me to come along and read some of my funny ones?"

"Yes, because I told her you write a lot, not just poems," agreed Lee.

"OK, well I got chatting with Miss Arthur afterwards and she was very interested about the book, asked me if she could have a sneak preview of some chapters and she really enjoyed them. Then she phoned and asked if she could email them to a friend of hers who's a journalist."

"And this is the person who wants to write an article now"? Tom asked.

"Yes" replied Annie, grinning widely "her name's Meg, we've talked on the phone and emailed for the past week and she knows about online publishing as well, so she's offered to help me. She also knows someone at the radio station, and they've asked if I'd to do that too."

"And you've kept it a secret all this time - no wonder you've been acting a bit weirder than usual lately" laughed

Aunt Lizzie, then she turned to Lee "and what a clever lad you are to have started all this!"

Lee grinned, looking almost embarrassed but very pleased with himself.

"Wow" exclaimed Jade "this is amazing, when are you doing these interviews, mum?"

"I'm doing the radio thing on Wednesday, then Meg is coming here on Saturday, she wants to meet all the mad characters in the book!" Annie replied with a smirk.

Her daughter looked panic stricken.

"So, I've only got about five days to get you ready?" she exclaimed.

Now it was Annie's turn to look worried.

"Oh no, my girl, you're not doing one of your makeovers on me – it's a radio show, so they only have to listen, not look."

"But there'll be a photographer for the article, surely" Aunt Lizzie pointed out.

Jade looked at Annie with a determined expression on her face.

"Right mum, we need to agree on you getting *something* done – haircut and colour at least."

Annie pondered this,

"Well, I suppose that doesn't involve any pain, so ok to that."

"Manicure?"

"Ok, that's fine too."

"How about having your eyelashes tinted?"

"Getting a bit carried away now, my girl."

"Ok, we'll come back to that nearer the time" Jade agreed reluctantly.

Annie heaved a sigh of relief until Jade spoke again,
"Oh, and one more thing mum."
"What now" Annie sighed.
"*Definitely* no Crocs!"

The next morning Kate called in for a coffee and Annie told her the news.

Her sister was thrilled but quite stunned at first, as she took in the sight of Annie standing knee deep in laundry, while at the same time stirring a pot of soup and flipping potato scones on the griddle.

"How can you be so calm and – well, almost normal?" asked Kate "shouldn't you at least be a bit nervous?"

"I was wondering about that myself" her sister replied "I just don't think it's really sunk in yet. In the meantime, life goes on and I still have to deal with all this."

Annie waved her arm to indicate the pile of ironing on the table and the sink overflowing with dishes.

"Aunt Lizzie had a dentist appointment this morning, she was ready to cancel it to help me out, but I wouldn't let her."

"I don't mind giving you a hand for an hour or so" offered Kate.

Annie gave her a hug.

"That's really good of you sis, but I think I need to keep busy, and doing this sort of stuff keeps me grounded as well, otherwise my imagination runs riot."

"Thinking of all the money you could make you mean?" laughed Kate.

"Well, it would be nice to earn a bob or two certainly," Annie grinned back at her "I doubt if it will be ponies and

Porsches kind of money – but maybe I could manage a couple of gerbils and a Jeep!"

CHAPTER THIRTY THREE

On the morning of the radio interview Annie still hadn't had an attack of nerves as such, but she did feel quite emotional. She had been thinking a lot about her mum over the past few days, wishing she was here and knowing how proud she would have been.

She had allowed Jade to organise her hair and nail appointments and Kate had persuaded her to buy a smart new jacket, Aunt Lizzie bought her a silk scarf to go with it, then Tom had presented her with a lovely pair of silver earrings. As if that wasn't enough, her dad had cycled along from the village just as she was about to leave, with a huge bouquet of flowers tied to his handlebars, which had reduced her to tears.

"I can't believe I'm all done up like this just to go on the radio," she said to Tom on the way into town "no-one is going to see me anyway."

"That's not the point," replied Tom "you look and sound really confident, and that will come across to the listeners."

"Wonder how I'd sound if I'd worn my waterproofs and wellies then."

The radio interview went really well, and Annie had thoroughly enjoyed it, especially when a number of listeners had phoned in while she was on air to say they'd be downloading the book as soon as it was available, which would be within the next week.

She'd also had loads of phone calls and emails from friends who had been amazed to hear her when they'd tuned in, because Annie had sworn the family to secrecy until it was over as she didn't want anyone else to know in advance, in case the thought made her nervous.

All that remained now was the interview with Meg which, unfortunately, would mean having photographs taken, but when she'd moaned about that to Jade, her daughter had been very unsympathetic and told her she'd just have to 'suck it up'.

On Saturday morning the rest of the family appeared to be suffering from the nerves that had still not affected Annie, which she found highly amusing.

Jade spent over an hour in the bathroom, causing a queue to form outside until Tom yelled at her to get a move on, then he himself changed his clothes twice before he was satisfied. Aunt Lizzie made a fuss over bathing Rory and dressing him in one of his best outfits and Lee was forced into having a shower and putting on smart trousers and a shirt, which he was very unhappy about. They were all clean and shiny by half past nine.

"This is a bit premature" Annie laughed, still wandering about in her pyjamas and dressing gown, "they're not coming till after one, for Pete's sake, what are you all going to do till then?"

"Never mind us," said Jade "when are *you* going to start getting ready?"

"Don't know yet, but I'm going to have an hour or so in the garden first."

"WHAT! Are you serious?" spluttered Tom.

"You can't mum, you'll ruin your nails."

"I'll wear my Marigolds."

"You need to shower and do your hair as well." said Aunt Lizzie.

"That will only take ten minutes."

"Trust me mum, it will take a lot longer than that to get your hair looking right."

"I was just going to leave it to dry on its own, like I usually do."

Jade took a deep breath, then said slowly,

"I will be blow drying your hair mother, even if I have to tie you to a chair, because you are *not* going to appear in this article looking like Worzel Gummidge."

Half an hour later Annie was in the garden.

She had insisted that the two boys be allowed to get back into old clothes and out in the garden for a couple of hours and Lee was greatly relieved.

Jade and Tom had also seen sense and changed into their old clothes for a while as well. Her daughter had slapped a thick layer of moisturising cream on her face and was now reading a magazine, sitting beside Aunt Lizzie who was knitting, as usual, while they both had their feet in the paddling pool.

Lee and Rory were chasing each other across the grass with giant water pistols, while Tom had offered to help Annie in the vegetable garden so they were now digging over the plot where they would plant potatoes.

"What time is your dad coming?" Tom asked.

"I told him about twelve would be time enough."

"Are you sure it's a good idea, who knows what he might say."

"He's one of the main characters Tom, of course he should be here."

"You do like to live life on the edge, don't you?" her husband said drily.

At around eleven thirty Annie finally decided she'd better start getting ready, especially since she'd forgotten to put her Marigolds on so it would take a bit of time to get her hands clean, but a bowl of bleach and soapy water usually did the trick.

She jabbed her fork into the soil one last time and bent over to shake the clump vigorously to free it of weeds. At the same moment she heard a horrible squelching noise and looked down to see a slug the size of a Cuban cigar oozing between her fingers.

Her screams rent the air, causing Sophie to take off like a rocket and dive into the bushes at the far end of the garden.

At the corner of the house Grandad, in his best suit and tie, stood watching for a moment then turned to the two women who had followed him down the lane in a four-wheel drive vehicle, one of whom was hastily setting up a video camera on a tripod.

"I don't think you know what you're letting yourself in for" he said grimly, as the second woman took in the sight of Tom helping his shuddering wife across the lawn.

She also saw an older woman wringing out her wet knitting, a teenage girl dunking her head in the paddling pool and scrubbing her face with a towel, while a boy on a skateboard, wearing a Sumo suit, hurtled along the path and a toddler weaved his way towards them with a spade that looked as if it had a large lump of soil on it.

"And as for that poor soul" Grandad continued, nodding across to where Sophie's quivering backside was sticking out from under the hedge,

"Well, I reckon if that dog had a suitcase, she'd have packed and bloody well gone by now."

Three days later Annie's book went online.

That evening, after a mentally and emotionally exhausting day, she poured herself a glass of wine and went to the study.

She sat by the window and stared out at the clouds drifting slowly across the sky until she saw what she was looking for.

Then, with tears in her eyes, Annie leant her head against the glass and whispered,

"I've done it mum, I've finally piggin' done it."

THE END

I saw my mum in a cloud today
And it made me shed a tear
I loved her more than words can say
And I wish she was still here

I wish that she was here again
To help when things go wrong
To gently fuss and offer me
A hug when I'm not strong

I wish she could have known the joy
Her five grandchildren brought
She only knew but two of them
Her time was cut so short

She would have loved them all, I know
The hugs, the laughs, the fun
The youngest now is nine years old
The eldest, twenty-one

I wondered though, perhaps she has
Been looking down some days
And seen it all and smiled on them
While watching them at play

My tears were falling fast and free
Then I smiled, because I think
That just before that cloud changed shape
I'm sure I saw her wink

Written 2003, in memory of my mum 1925 – 1986

Printed in Poland
by Amazon Fulfillment
Poland Sp. z o.o., Wrocław

61091703R00112